The Hot & Cold Summer

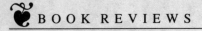 # BOOK REVIEWS

Here's what people are saying:

With an assist from Owen's nifty drawings, Hurwitz scores again.

from PUBLISHERS WEEKLY

The adventures of the three move along quickly, and the characters are developed quite well for such a brief novel. The scenes are realistic and are particularly effective in depicting the problems of a triangular friendship.

from SCHOOL LIBRARY JOURNAL

This episodic novel is cheerful and perceptive—right on target for both boys and girls.

from THE BOOKLIST

Honored with the Parent's Choice Award

Books presents

The Hot & Cold Summer

Johanna Hurwitz
illustrated by Gail Owens

William Morrow and Company
New York • 1984

*For my lifelong friend,
made through propinquity and
retained through affection,
Lillian Webb*

This book is a presentation of
Weekly Reader Books.
Weekly Reader Books offers book clubs for children
from preschool through junior high school.

For further information write to:
Weekly Reader Books
4343 Equity Drive
Columbus, Ohio 43228

Edited for Weekly Reader Books and published
by arrangement with William Morrow and Company.

Printed in the United States of America.

Library of Congress Cataloging in Publication Data
Hurwitz, Johanna.   The hot and cold summer.
Summary: Two inseparable ten-year-old boys discover there is room in
their friendship for another person and it really doesn't matter that she is
a girl.
[1. Friendship—Fiction] I. Owens, Gail, ill. II. Title. PZ7.H9574Ho
1984   [Fic]   83-19336
ISBN 0–688–02746–6

Book design by Cindy Simon

Contents

1
Propinquity???!

Whenever you saw Rory Dunn walking down the street or riding his bicycle, he was with Derek Curry. The boys were best friends and always seemed to be together.

Rory, whose real name was Richard (but no one ever called him that except his grandmother), had dark brown hair and wore glasses. Derek was much taller than Rory and had curly blond hair.

The differences in their appearance were not the only differences the boys had. Rory was bossy and liked to make all the decisions for himself and his friend. But Derek didn't seem to mind. They got along just fine. "You'd think they were brothers," their neighbor, Mrs. Golding, often said. That showed how little Mrs. Golding knew. Brothers and sisters fight with one another. Rory and Derek never quarreled, from the moment they met on the way to school in the morning till the end of the day when they said good-bye. Half the time during the week, Rory wound up eating dinner at Derek's house. And the other evenings, Derek found himself sitting around the table with Rory's family.

"What a joy to see such good friends," Mrs. Golding would say with a smile.

Mrs. Golding saw a great deal of the boys. Her home on Dogleg Lane in Woodside, New Jersey, was right between Rory's house and Derek's house. If anything could be said to come between the two boys, it was the Goldings' house. Luckily the Goldings were easygoing people and didn't complain when the boys, at a very young age, started taking a shortcut through their backyard when they went out to play. Before long, there was a well-worn path through the Goldings' grass as well as a hole in the hedges on either side of their property. But Mr. Golding could remember back to his own younger days, and he knew that the twenty seconds or so the boys saved by using his yard was very important.

Rory and Derek had known each other since they were three years old. Neither of them could remember a time before the Currys moved to the street where the Dunn family already lived. There were only six weeks separating the boys in age. So from May 4 they were always the same age until the following March when Rory was once again temporarily older than his friend. This year the boys were ten years old and they had just finished fourth grade. Some years they were in the same classroom in the Woodside Elementary School. There were four sections of each grade and the teachers liked to mix everyone up so that they would make new friends. But it didn't matter whether Rory and Derek were in the same room or not. Nothing could separate them or change their friendship, not even being assigned to different classrooms.

"Your friendship is a matter of propinquity," Rory's father had once told his son.

"Pro-what?" asked Rory.

"Pro-pin-quity," said his father, slowly sounding out the word. Mr. Dunn taught English at the Woodside Middle School, and he often used big words to enrich his son's vocabulary. "It means that your friendship with Derek has developed because of the nearness of our home to his. If we had moved a couple of blocks away or to a different community, you guys wouldn't know each other at all."

Rory didn't agree. He was sure that wherever they lived, he and Derek would have met and been friends. Propinquity, or whatever it was called, only made life more convenient for them. And since it was now summer vacation and they lived so close to each other, it meant that they had even more time to play.

Rory liked knowing that for the next two months no teacher would tell him what to do. He didn't have to think about arithmetic homework or book reports or spelling quizzes. Instead, he and Derek could read comics or go swimming or practice basketball shots whenever they wanted. Derek's mother had suggested that the boys go off to a sleep-away camp for two weeks during the vacation.

"A change is always stimulating," she had said.

But Rory didn't want to go. He didn't need a change. He liked things just as they were. The last big change in his life had been when his sister Edna was born, which showed how unnecessary changes could be. So Rory convinced Derek that he should refuse to go to camp, too. "We don't need new experiences or camp counselors ordering us about," he told Derek. And because Derek was a good friend, he agreed with Rory.

On the first day of summer vacation, the boys were sitting under the maple tree in

Derek's yard rereading all their old comic books. Between them, they owned close to two hundred. There was *Spiderman*, *The Amazing Hulk*, *Superman*, and a lot of others. Even though they had read them many times before, Rory enjoyed rereading them over and over.

Suddenly Mrs. Golding stuck her head through the hole in the hedge and called to the boys, "I have wonderful news!" Her face was red with excitement.

Rory looked at Derek and smiled. Derek returned the smile with a knowing look. The flushed face and the broad smile probably meant that Mrs. Golding had been making cookies. She often did.

"I didn't want to tell you until I was sure," she continued. "But I just had a phone call from my niece and the plan has been all worked out."

Rory looked puzzled. Could Mrs. Golding's niece have given her a new cookie recipe over the telephone? It seemed unlikely.

"What is it?" he asked suspiciously. He didn't mind having his reading interrupted for chocolate chip cookies. But somehow, he suspected that Mrs. Golding hadn't been baking at all.

"You know my niece and her husband are archeologists?" began Mrs. Golding.

The boys nodded their heads. They had read about an archeologist in one of the comic books. Was it Superman who had come to his rescue or Spiderman?

"Well, this summer they are going to Turkey on a dig."

Neither Rory nor Derek felt the excitement that Mrs. Golding did from this news. They had both heard their neighbor speaking about her niece in the past, but it wasn't something that really concerned them. Rory picked up the Superman comic that he had been reading and held it open. He didn't care about someone else's relatives.

"Turkey's pretty far away, isn't it?" asked Derek. He had no idea where it was, and he imagined it as a country where thousands of chickens and turkeys marched up and down the streets.

"That's exactly what I told my niece. It's too far away and what will she do there all day long while you're digging? So, I said, why doesn't she spend the summer here. She can play with you boys and have a wonderful time. And that way her parents won't have to worry about her at all," Mrs. Golding concluded, the blood rushing to her face again.

"If she's an archeologist, why won't they let her dig?" asked Derek. Mrs. Golding wasn't making any sense.

"She wouldn't want to play with us," said Rory.

"Of course she would. She's just your age. You'll love her. I know you will. So I've been trying to convince my niece for weeks, and just now she phoned and agreed. So it's all worked out. I'm so happy."

"What's worked out?" asked Rory.

"Who will we love?" asked Derek.

"Why, Bolivia, of course!" said Mrs. Golding. "That's who I've been talking about."

"Bolivia?" Derek said, puzzled. "That's a country."

"I think we studied about it," said Rory. "It's far away, like Turkey."

"I really don't know the distance," said Mrs. Golding, shrugging her shoulders. "I guess I could check on a map. It *is* a strange name for a girl, but her mother had just finished a course in pre-Columbian archeology."

"I don't understand," said Rory.

"Neither do I," said Derek.

"It's very simple," said Mrs. Golding. "Bolivia is coming here. She's not a country. She's a girl!"

"Is that your niece?" asked Rory.

"Of course not," said Mrs. Golding. "I told you my niece is going to Turkey. Bolivia is her daughter. She's my great-niece, and she's going to spend the summer right here in

Woodside while her parents are away. What good times you all will have."

Rory looked at Derek. Their plans for the summer did not include Mrs. Golding's great-niece. "The whole summer?" he asked.

"Yes. I'm so happy. You'll see. Bolivia is smart as a whip," said Mrs. Golding. "She's an *A* student at her school in upstate New York. I know you'll like her."

Rory knew he wouldn't, but he couldn't tell his neighbor that. Instead he said, "How old is she?"

"I told you. She's just your age. She was ten in February."

Rory winced. He was small for his age, and because both his parents were short, he knew that he would probably always be short himself, shorter than Derek anyway. Being six weeks older than Derek made up for that. It made him feel good that although Derek was bigger, he was older. Now someone was coming along who was going to be older than he. He was sure that she would be taller, too. Most kids he knew were taller than he was unless they were very young. And worst of all, she was a girl.

"I've got to go inside and start making arrangements," said Mrs. Golding. "I want to empty out the closet in the guest room and bake some cookies for when Bolivia arrives."

For once Rory wasn't at all interested in Mrs. Golding's cookies. As soon as their neighbor had gone back into her house, he began complaining.

"What a stupid name," said Rory. "We don't need that Bolivia coming here."

'Well, maybe she won't be too bad,' said Derek hopefully. "We haven't met her yet."

"She's a girl, isn't she?" demanded Rory. "I know all about girls. Don't forget I've got a sister."

"Yeah, but Edna is only three years old," reminded Derek. "Bolivia is our age. So maybe it won't be so bad after all."

"Believe me, it will be awful," said Rory with certainty. "Suppose Traci or Erin or Kathleen were going to be living next door to us all summer long," he said, rattling off the names of girls they knew at school.

"Yeah. I guess you're right," said Derek. "But still, we have to be nice."

"No way," said Rory. "We didn't invite her here. I think we should just ignore her. We can pretend she doesn't exist."

"You mean we won't talk to her? We'll pretend that we don't see her?" asked Derek.

"Exactly," agreed Rory. He held out his hand. "Swear that you'll never speak to her," he said to Derek.

"I swear," said Derek, solemnly shaking hands with Rory. "Mrs. Golding will get angry at us," he said a moment later.

"So what," said Rory. "It's her own fault. Who asked her to have her stupid niece come here? She should have gone to Turkey and eaten turkey with her parents."

"Gobble, gobble, gobble," said Derek.

"Right," agreed Rory. "Gobble, gobble."

It was hard for Rory to get absorbed in the comic books again because he kept thinking about the intruder. "We didn't find out when she's coming," he said after a few minutes.

"Who?" asked Derek.

"Gobble, gobble."

Derek put down a Spiderman comic book and looked for an older issue he hadn't reread recently.

"Boys," a voice shouted at them from the house next door. It was Mrs. Golding sticking her head out of the guest-room window. "I forgot to tell you something."

"What?" they asked.

"Guess what Bolivia is bringing with her?"

"A turkey," said Rory.

"Her dolls?" asked Derek.

"It's a wonderful surprise for us all," said Mrs. Golding. "Bolivia is bringing Lucette with her."

Mrs. Golding didn't wait for a response. She pulled her head back inside the window and returned to her cleaning.

Derek looked at Rory.

Rory looked at Derek. "If there is one thing worse than having a girl come and stay next door to you all summer," he said, "it's two girls!"

Derek shrugged his shoulders. "Gobble, gobble," he said.

2
Hiding

The following Tuesday, Rory and Derek sat down to supper in the Dunns' kitchen. Tuesday was the evening that Derek's father, who was a dentist, had late hours for his patients. Derek's mother worked with her husband, so Derek always spent Tuesday evening with Rory. Usually their meals together were a lot of fun for the boys, but not tonight.

"Mrs. Golding tells me that Boliva will be arriving tomorrow," said Rory's mother.

Rory didn't respond.

"I think it's wonderful that she is the same age as you boys," Mrs. Dunn went on. "You can all play together and have a wonderful time."

That was too much for Rory. "We don't

need her," he said, putting down his fork. "Derek and I don't need anyone else. Besides," he said, "I don't like girls."

"Of course, you do," insisted his father. "You like Edna."

Edna was three years old. She smiled, delighted to hear herself referred to.

"I like Rory," she said. "And I like Derek, too."

"Great," said Rory. "You can like Bolivia, too, for all I care. You can play with her. Not me."

"Bolivia. Bolivia," said Edna, trying out the name.

Rory looked at his sister with distaste. Edna had watched Rory and Derek putting ketchup on their French fries. Then she had taken the ketchup bottle and poured the red ketchup not only on her potatoes but on her meat loaf and her string beans. It was a wonder she didn't flavor her milk with it, too, while she was at it, thought Rory.

"I'll play with Bolivia," agreed Edna.

"Shut up and eat your ketchup," said Rory.

"Rory. Don't talk like that to your sister," Mrs. Dunn scolded.

"Come, Edna. Eat your meat loaf," Mrs. Dunn said in a much gentler tone, as she spooned some of the ketchup off Edna's plate.

14

Derek ate silently. He didn't have any brothers or sisters, and Rory knew Edna didn't bother him at all. But Derek didn't have to live with her all day long.

"I want you boys to be friendly to Bolivia," said Mrs. Dunn, returning to her earlier subject. "She won't know any other children in town. It's going to be up to you to see that she has a good time in Woodside."

"She didn't have to come here," said Rory. "She could have gone to Turkey. Anyway, we didn't invite her. I don't see why Derek and I have to be stuck with her." He paused a moment, thinking of a new word that his father had taught him recently. "She's *superfluous*," he said, proud to have remembered.

"It's the decent way to behave," said Mr. Dunn. "Now, listen," he said. "I have a wonderful plan. Tomorrow evening Derek's parents will be home. So I'm going to have a cookout in the backyard and invite the Goldings and the Currys. That way, Bolivia will get to meet us all and you can get acquainted."

"Derek and I won't be around for supper tomorrow night," said Rory, thinking fast.

"Is that so?" asked his mother with surprise. Derek looked surprised, too. This was the first he knew about it.

"Where will you be?" asked Mrs. Dunn.

"I told you we were going to Maurice's house."

"You did?" said Mrs. Dunn.

"You never listen to me," complained Rory.

Maurice was a boy who had been in the same fourth-grade class as Rory. The reason that Rory thought of his name now was that of all the kids he knew, Maurice lived the farthest away. If Bolivia was coming tomorrow, it was important to be as far from the scene as possible. Rory would explain that to Derek later.

"Well, try and make it back in time for supper tomorrow," said Mrs. Dunn with a frown. "I bought a bag of marshmallows to toast over the fire," she added.

"I want a marshmallow," Edna whined. "Give me a marshmallow now."

Rory slipped away from the table as his mother attempted to explain to Edna that the treats were for the next evening. "Come on." He gestured to Derek. "Let's get out of here before we have to watch Edna eating marshmallows covered with ketchup."

"I don't want ketchup on them. I just want a plain marshmallow," insisted Edna as the boys left the house.

"What's the story with Maurice?" asked Derek as soon as they got outside.

"Look," said Rory. "I hate being told that

we have to be friends with this Bolivia. It isn't fair. I don't tell my mother who she should be friends with. No one tells me that I have to play with you," he said, looking at Derek. "I bet if my mother said that I had to play with you, I'd hate you."

"How could you hate me?" asked Derek. "I'm your best friend."

"You're my best friend because I want you to be my best friend. Not because my mother says I have to play with you."

Derek slowly nodded his head in understanding. "I see what you mean," he said.

"So, tomorrow we're going to Maurice's house," said Rory.

"Okay." Derek sighed. "But he's awfully boring."

"Never mind. We can't stay around here. And we have to stay there until after supper," Rory explained.

"You mean we can't ever come home now that this Bolivia is coming?" asked Derek.

"Well, if we don't meet her, we can't play with her," said Rory.

"That's going to be pretty hard," said Derek. "Do you think they'll save some marshmallows for us?"

If Maurice was surprised to have Derek and Rory show up at his house first thing on

Wednesday morning, he didn't say anything.

"I'm going to sort out my stamp collection today," he said. "You guys can help."

It wasn't the kind of activity that Rory ordinarily enjoyed. But today he was willing to do anything that would keep them far away from home.

Maurice pulled a shopping bag out of his closet. It was filled with stamps. "I've been saving them in here all year," he explained. "Now that I've got time, I'm going to arrange them by country."

The boys each took a handful of stamps and started arranging them in piles: United States, Canada, Great Britain, France. . . .

It was very boring and seemed a lot like schoolwork.

"Do you want to play frisbee or something?" asked Rory after a while. His neck was stiff from bending over the stamps.

"It's too hot," said Maurice, and he kept on sorting stamps.

"Do you think you mother would drive us over to the pool?" asked Derek. He and Rory had worn swimming trunks under their shorts, just in case.

"I'm getting over a cold and I can't go to the pool till next week," said Maurice.

Rory and Derek could have just gotten up and said good-bye, but that would have spoiled Rory's plan. So they kept on sorting stamps.

Finally it was lunchtime. Maurice's mother invited them to stay. That had also been part of their plan. Maurice's mother served sandwiches made with little squiggly things called sprouts. "We eat a lot of health food around here," said Maurice, biting into his sandwich. Personally, Rory thought that peanut butter was a healthy food. It certainly tasted more interesting than what they were eating. The sprouts reminded Rory of mealworms. They had fed mealworms to a frog at school last year, and Rory found he had to close his eyes before he could bring himself to bite into his sandwich. It helped a little, but not much.

He remembered that they wanted to be invited for supper, too. "This is great," he said politely as he tried to hide part of his sandwich in his pocket to dispose of later. "I bet you have great things for supper, too."

"Tonight we're having vegetable burgers," said Maurice's mother, as she set out dishes of yogurt and sprinkled wheat germ on top.

Rory's stomach turned a somersault. "I'm pretty full," he said, pushing aside his dish of yogurt.

"Me, too," said Derek.

The boys returned to Maurice's room and to the stamps. It seemed endless.

"Where did you get so many stamps?" asked Derek.

"My cousin used to collect stamps, but he gave up on it and gave them all to me," said Maurice.

Rory thought that Maurice's cousin seemed like a pretty sensible guy.

Maurice's mother stuck her head into the room. "I'm going shopping," she said. "I'll be back in a couple of hours." She turned to Derek and Rory. "If you boys would like to stay for supper, we'll be glad to have you. Just call your mothers and tell them."

Derek and Rory nodded. They had already planned to stay for supper at Maurice's house, but that was before they'd known about the vegetable burgers.

As the afternoon dragged on, Derek suggested they turn on the TV.

"Sorry," said Maurice. "I'm not allowed to watch it before supper."

He looked at his watch. "It's time for me to practice now anyhow," he said. He went to his closet and took out his violin case.

"You can be my audience. It's good experience to play before an audience," he said.

Maurice started to play a melody from *Carmen*. Rory and Derek recognized it because Maurice had played it in the assembly just before school ended. He had played it in the

classroom during the term. He had also played it at the assembly the year before. It was probably the only thing he knew how to play, and he didn't even play it very well. Rory didn't know too much about music, but he could tell when a wrong note was played because every time Maurice made a mistake, he stamped his foot and said, "Darn."

"How long do you have to practice?" asked Derek.

"Only forty-five minutes," said Maurice.

"Darn," said Rory under his breath. "I'll be right back." He went to the bathroom where he flushed the remains of his sprout-and-tofu sandwich down the toilet.

When he returned, Maurice was starting to play the piece all over again.

He hit another wrong note and stamped his foot. "Darn!"

"I think we're making you nervous," said Derek. "We'll wait out in your yard." The two boys rushed outside before Maurice could insist again that he needed the experience of playing before an audience.

"Let's go home," begged Derek. "How bad can that girl Bolivia be?"

"Bad," said Rory firmly. "Very bad. We're staying right here."

"She can't be as bad as sprouts and *Carmen*

and arranging stamps all day long," said Derek. "I feel like I work in a post office."

"If we go home, it will be worse," said Rory.

"I don't believe it," said his friend.

"In the first place," said Rory, "we can always go home. But if we go home now, we're really stuck. Bolivia is going to be around all summer. She's going to want to go wherever we go and do whatever we do. And, what's worse, our parents are on her side."

"Where will we go tomorrow?" asked Derek in a resigned tone. "I don't want to come back here."

"We could spend a day at the library," suggested Rory.

"A whole day?"

"We could go to the movies and sit through the picture three times," said Rory. He thought a moment. "If necessary, we could run away from home."

"That's crazy," said Derek. "Why should we have to run away from home? This is our vacation. We should be able to do what we want."

"Right," said Rory. "That's what I've been saying all along. How about if we go home and just ignore her?"

"Right," said Derek.

"If we ignore her when she follows us around, she'll get bored. She won't want to play with us. And then we'll be free of her," Rory reasoned.

"Right," said Derek. It seemed an easy enough plan to follow.

"Besides," said Rory. "My mother's making that cookout tonight with real meat hamburgers."

"You mean there won't be any sprouts?" asked Derek.

"Right," said Rory. "And marshmallows, too," he remembered.

"What are we waiting for?" asked Derek. "Let's go."

"Right," said Rory. "But we won't talk to Bolivia," he reminded his friend again. "We'll just act as if she isn't there."

"Right," agreed Derek.

They went back into Maurice's house to tell him that there was a change in their plans.

"Aren't you going to help me with the stamps anymore?" asked Maurice. "I've got two more bags in my closet."

"Sorry," said Rory, remembering to be polite. Another day he might be very glad to hide out in Maurice's house again, even if it meant sorting stamps.

3
The Barbecue

Rory and Derek slowly rode their bikes back to Dogleg Lane.

"Remember, don't talk to her at all," Rory said one more time.

Derek nodded. "Did you ever find out who Lucette is?" he asked.

"Who?"

"The girl she's bringing with her. Don't you remember, Mrs. Golding said she was bringing Lucette."

"Oh, her," answered Rory. "It's probably a little sister like Edna. Maybe she'll have to stay around and help take care of her."

"You're right," agreed Derek as they neared their street. "Lucette must be her little sister. I'm surprised her parents didn't name her Hong Kong or something."

They got off their bikes and left them in Rory's driveway.

"I'm home!" Rory shouted.

Mrs. Dunn came out of the kitchen. She smiled at the boys. "I'm glad you made it back in time for the cookout," she said. "Edna and I are just finishing the cole slaw."

Rory looked in the kitchen and saw his sister sitting on a high stool by the counter trying to slice some cabbage with a dull butter knife.

"I made the potato salad, too," Edna bragged.

"Your father is going to start the fire in a few minutes," Mrs. Dunn told Rory. "I met Bolivia when the Goldings brought her from the airport. She seems like a lovely girl."

Rory just shrugged his shoulders.

"I like Lucette," said Edna.

"Wait till you see Lucette," said Mrs. Dunn. "You boys are really in for a treat."

That was too much for Rory and Derek. They ran out to the backyard to see if they could help with the fire.

By five-thirty the fire was blazing, and Edna had convinced her mother to give her just one marshmallow. Mrs. Dunn was setting out the bowls of cole slaw and potato salad.

Derek's parents came over bringing a cake box. "Oh, Janet, you didn't have to do that," said Rory's mother.

"I picked it up at the new bakery on my way

home from work," said Mrs. Curry. "It looked too good to leave there. I'm sure it will get eaten."

Derek and Rory grinned at one another. The cake, the hamburgers, and the bottle of root beer that was waiting on the table were the least that they should get in compensation for Bolivia. The boys waited, knowing the two girls would emerge from behind the Goldings' hedge at any moment.

Sure enough, the hedge parted and first Mr. and then Mrs. Golding and then a redheaded girl walked into the Dunns' yard. "This is Bolivia!" said Mrs. Golding proudly. She said it in the same way she often introduced a new type of cookie or cake, as if Bolivia were something she had created in her kitchen. Rory took a quick look and then shifted his gaze. He didn't want to appear interested. He noticed, however, that he had been right about one thing. Bolivia was several inches taller than he was.

"Hi, Bolivia. Welcome to Woodside!" said Mr. Dunn. "I'm just putting on the hamburgers. How do you like yours?"

"I like mine rare," said Bolivia.

"Fine," said Mr. Dunn. "So do Rory and Derek." He turned to the boys, who were trying to edge away from the guest of honor. Derek's mother grabbed him. "Bolivia, this is

Derek. He and Rory will be your friends this summer."

Neither boy said anything.

"How's Lucette settling in?" asked Mrs. Dunn. Rory realized for the first time that Bolivia's little sister hadn't come to the barbecue.

"She's fine. At first she was very quiet, but just before we left the house she said her first word to me. She knows ten words. It's so exciting," said Mrs. Golding.

Bolivia turned to Rory and Derek. "I couldn't bring Lucette to the barbecue because the smoke might be bad for her," she explained. "Do you want to come to my aunt's house and see her?"

These were the first words Bolivia spoke directly to the boys.

Rory shook his head no. Derek also shook his head.

"Don't be shy," said Mr. Golding. "Go meet Lucette."

Rory shook his head again.

"You fellows are missing something really special," said Mrs. Dunn as she removed the plastic wrap from the salads.

Rory couldn't understand his mother. Why should he get excited over someone else's baby sister? He didn't care that Lucette had said her first word. Edna had known a lot of words by the time she was two. What was so special about Lucette?

Derek leaned toward Rory and whispered, "If we keep our mouths full of food, we can't talk."

Rory grinned. If his mother had told him once, she had told him a thousand times not to talk with food in his mouth.

"Right." He nodded.

The boys picked up paper plates. "Can we start eating?" asked Rory.

"If you're so hungry that you can't wait, go ahead," said Mrs. Dunn. Both boys piled their plates with potato salad and cole slaw.

Bolivia picked up a plate, too.

Edna pulled on Bolivia's skirt. "I made the cole slaw," she said.

"No kidding," said Bolivia.

"I made the potato salad, too," said Edna.

"The rare burgers are ready," called Mr. Dunn.

The three older children went to get their meat.

"You know," Bolivia said, turning to Rory and Derek, "last summer I was in Israel with my parents. They make hamburgers out of turkey there."

It was hard to imagine turkey hamburgers, although Rory thought they probably would be better than vegetable burgers with sprouts.

"Gobble, gobble," said Derek.

"What?" asked Bolivia.

"Gobble, gobble," he repeated.

Rory kicked Derek. His friend wasn't exactly speaking to Bolivia, but it was close.

Derek got the message. He stuffed his mouth with potato salad.

"Do you like my potato salad?" asked Edna.

"Rory, tell Bolivia about Woodside. This is her first visit here," Mr. Dunn called from his position at the grill.

Rory shoveled in a large forkful of potato salad and turned to his father, pointing to his mouth.

"There's a lot of things to do around here," said Mrs. Curry, since neither of the boys were speaking. "There's the town pool." She turned to Derek. "Which are the days when the public library is showing free movies for kids?" she asked.

Derek took an enormous bite out of his hamburger and shrugged his shoulders.

Rory licked some ketchup off his fingers and went back to refill his plate. Luckily he was very hungry after the lunch at Maurice's house.

"You like my cole slaw?" asked Edna.

"Where else have you traveled with your parents?" asked Mrs. Dunn.

Good, thought Rory. Let the grown-ups keep Bolivia busy talking. She sounded like a

30

geography book, listing all the foreign countries where she'd been: Israel, Egypt, Mexico, France, Spain. . . .

After a little while, Bolivia turned to the boys again. "Would you like to come over tomorrow and play with Lucette?" she asked. "We could teach her some new words. I'll let you feed her if you like."

Girls really have no idea what boys like to do, Rory thought. What boy in his right mind would want to sit around playing nursery school with a little baby? He shook his head no.

"How about you?" asked Bolivia, turning to Derek.

"No," said Derek. Then realizing what he had done, he pushed another forkful of potato salad into his mouth.

Bolivia sat down on the ground next to Edna. She began playing "This little piggy went to market" on the little girl's bare toes. It was probably the eighty thousandth time that someone had played that baby game with Edna, but still she laughed and laughed.

Rory moved away, taking Derek with him.

"Boys, don't rush off," shouted Mrs. Curry. "We're going to cut the cake soon."

Bolivia was not going to scare them off the cake, Rory decided. Especially since it had chocolate frosting. So the boys moved back to the center of activity. Mrs. Golding was busy discussing something with the two mothers. Mr. Golding, the neighborhood authority when it came to cars, was talking to Mr. Dunn and Mr. Curry about motors.

Rory saw Bolivia go through the hedge back to the Goldings' house. Maybe she had to use the bathroom, he thought. But just maybe, she was getting the message that he and Derek didn't want her around.

With Bolivia gone, at least for a few minutes, the boys could stop eating and rest. It was hard work keeping your mouth stuffed with food.

"What should we do tomorrow?" asked Derek.

"Let's go to the pool," said Rory. "Mrs. Golding never signs up for a pool card and so Bolivia won't be allowed in."

"What if it rains?" asked Derek.

Rory looked up at the sky. It was still light and there wasn't a single cloud. "It won't rain," he said. "But if it does, we'll go over to Maurice's again."

"Okay," said Derek. "But if we go, I'm taking ear plugs with me. I've heard enough of that *Carmen*."

Rory stuck his hand into his pocket and pulled out a sprout from the sandwich he had disposed of earlier in the day. "A souvenir of the first afternoon hiding from Bolivia," he said, presenting it to Derek.

"This is just the beginning of July," said Derek. "Do you realize how many more days there are till she goes home?"

"As many days as there were sprouts in that sandwich," said Rory, sighing.

"It's going to be a long, long summer," agreed Derek.

At any other time, the thought of a long, long summer would have filled the boys with delight. But now it stretched endlessly before them.

4
Lucette Up a Tree

The morning after the barbecue, Derek and Rory met outside at nine-thirty. The boys wore their trunks under their clothes and each had a towel and a sandwich. Mrs. Dunn called after them, "Ask Bolivia to go with you," but Rory pretended not to hear. He had no intention of knocking on the Goldings' door. Anyway, Bolivia wouldn't have a membership card to the pool yet. And Rory didn't know if she had a bike. He didn't want to go anywhere with that girl and especially not if he had to go on foot. He looked around and was relieved that she was not in sight. He glanced up at the window of Bolivia's room and for a second, he thought he saw one of the curtains move. But then all was still again. It was probably just a little breeze.

"Let's get going," he said to Derek, who

had been checking the air in his tires. "We want to make our getaway while the coast is clear."

Suddenly the boys heard a shriek.

"Help, help! Lucette has escaped!"

Derek and Rory looked at each other. What was the big fuss? Had Bolivia's little sister climbed out of her playpen or something?

Bolivia stuck her head out of the upstairs window. "Have you seen Lucette?" she called.

The boys shook their heads. How could little Lucette manage the heavy door? "She's got to be inside the house," said Derek.

"No. I saw her go out the window," Bolivia shouted.

Rory dropped his bike in surprise. How could the baby get out the window?

"Go around the back," demanded Bolivia. "I'll come and look with you. She must be in one of the trees."

Derek and Rory stood stunned. Had Bolivia lost her senses? If the baby had fallen out the window, she would be lying on the ground. It was impossible that she would land in a tree.

Mrs. Golding came running out of the house. "Should we call the fire department?" she asked her niece.

"Call an ambulance or the police," said

Rory. His heart was beating loud. He knew how he would have felt if Edna had fallen out the window.

Mr. Golding had gone out the back door. "I see her. I see her," he called from the back-yard, "She's in the Dunns' mimosa tree."

Rory ran to the back of his house followed by Derek, Bolivia, and Mrs. Golding. He couldn't see any baby in the tree. "Where is she?" he shouted to Mr. Golding. He wondered if she had fallen out the window and then climbed the tree. It seemed incredible. He and Derek had been trying to climb that tree for years.

"It's all my fault." Bolivia was crying. "I opened the door so she could walk on my arm, and the next thing I knew she was flying around and around the room."

"She must be scared in a new place," said Mrs. Golding, putting her arm around her niece. "Don't cry. We'll all help catch her."

"I'll get a ladder," said Mr. Golding.

Rory watched as the old man leaned his ladder against the side of the tree.

"Hey, look at that!" shouted Derek.

Rory looked where his friend was pointing. On the very topmost brank of the mimosa tree was a large green bird with a blue-and-red head.

"It's a parrot!" he shouted. He had never

seen one before except in the encyclopedia, but there was no mistaking that size or color.

"Of course it's a parrot," Bolivia shouted at him. "What did you think Lucette was? An elephant?"

It wasn't only their vow of silence that kept Rory and Derek from admitting they had thought Lucette was a baby.

While they were shouting, the bird flew from the mimosa tree to the maple.

No sooner had the ladder been put in place there than the bird flew over the hedge and into the next yard, landing in a locust tree. Mr. Golding looked red in the face from the exertion of moving the ladder back and forth.

"Let me help," called Mr. Dunn, coming from the house. Twice a week, even during the summer, he took classes in school administration so that he might someday become a principal. Now he forgot his courses as he dropped his attaché case with his papers and books and ran toward Mr.Golding.

"Hello there. Hello there," shrieked Lucette as she flew from tree to tree.

"Hello there, yourself!" Derek called back. He looked at Rory. Rory hadn't told him not to speak to a bird.

Mrs. Dunn came outside, followed by Edna. The little girl began jumping up and down. "I see her!" she shouted. "Catch her. Catch her!"

"Hello there!" Lucette called down to them.

"I'm going to call the fire department," Mr. Golding said. "They have taller ladders, and we have an awful lot of trees around here for Lucette to investigate."

"Hello there!" Edna called up to the bird.

Mrs. Dunn put her arms around Bolivia. "Don't worry. We won't let her get away." She comforted the girl as Lucette flew into the branches of one tree and then another. The swimming pool was forgotten as Rory and Derek chased in and out of the hedges, keeping their eyes on the bird.

"Could we get her down with some food?" asked Derek when he stopped to catch his breath. "What does she like to eat?"

"Fruit," said Bolivia.

Everyone rushed home except the two men with the ladder. Rory brought back some grapes. Derek had an apple. "Hello there!" shouted Edna, waving a banana for Lucette.

They made a pile of all the fruit in the Golding yard. Lucette hovered in the air above it for a moment, but she didn't land.

"What else does she like?" asked Mrs. Dunn. "This isn't working."

Mr. Dunn climbed down the ladder as the

bird flew off once again. "None of my courses in running a school have prepared me for a morning like this," he said, wiping the sweat off his forehead.

In the distance they could hear approaching sirens. The fire department was on its way.

Dogleg Lane was filled with onlookers. People driving by got out of their cars to see what was happening. Neighbors came out of doors. Three large fire trucks pulled up in front of the Golding house. The firemen, wearing their helmets and tall boots, leaped off the trucks dragging ladders and long hoses with them.

"My vegetables could use a little water," said Mr. Dunn from where he was stationed.

"There's no fire," shouted Mrs. Golding. "It's a bird in the tree."

"Birds belong in trees," said one of the firemen, not yet understanding that Lucette was a pet bird who belonged in a cage.

"Hello there. Hello there!" Lucette greeted the new arrivals. She seemed to be having a great time.

Rory looked over at Bolivia. She was smiling. She looked like she was having a great time, too. For someone who had been crying a few minutes ago, she didn't seem unhappy now. Either she had wonderful faith in the

Woodside Fire Department or she was not really worried about the bird.

"Music!" Bolivia remembered suddenly. "Lucette loves country music."

Derek ran into his house and came out with the little transistor radio he had gotten on his last birthday. He fiddled with the dials, looking for a station that played country music.

"That's good," shouted Bolivia. "Leave it there."

Derek stood holding his radio at full volume and looking up at Lucette.

"Hello there," shouted the bird, swooping lower.

Strains of "Country Roads" came over the radio. The neighbors that had crowded around began to sing and clap their hands in time to the music.

Mrs. Golding began introducing Bolivia to the people that she recognized. Bolivia smiled at everyone. She was really enjoying this commotion very much, Rory decided.

"Can your parrot do any tricks?" asked one of the onlookers.

"She knows ten words and she can play dead and she comes flying to my arm when I call her," said Bolivia proudly.

She noticed Rory standing nearby listening

and added hastily, "But she won't come now. She's in a new place and she's overexcited by all the people."

The firemen got a call on their radio. There was a real fire somewhere. As quickly as they arrived, they disappeared with their sirens wailing. "We'll come back later if you still need us," one of the men called back as they departed.

Lucette seemed to be getting tired. She wasn't flying so much. She sat in the Currys' maple tree and looked around her.

"Who's my bird?" shouted Bolivia.

"Lucette. Lucette," the bird answered.

"Hey, she knows her name!" shouted Derek.

Rory was as excited by the bird as Derek. But he also had a strong suspicion that the whole morning had been planned by Bolivia. The more he thought about it, the more certain he was that she had opened the cage and the window on purpose. She had probably seen him through her window as he waited for Derek and she had decided to mess up the morning for them.

"I've got her. I've got her," shouted Mr. Dunn in triumph, as he slowly came down the ladder.

"Hello there!" Lucette greeted all the people in the yard. Everyone burst into applause and ran to get a closer look at the bird. The Goldings looked exhausted and relieved that this first emergency was over. Mr. Dunn handed Lucette over to Bolivia, looking very pleased with himself. It wasn't every morning that he climbed into trees to catch a bird.

"I feel like Tarzan," he said to Mrs. Dunn.

Derek just couldn't keep from asking Bolivia questions. "Where did you get her?" he wanted to know. "How many words can she say? Could she learn my name?" He was thrilled that Lucette was this clever bird and not the baby sister he and Rory had expected.

"You naughty girl," Bolivia scolded her pet. "I'm going to put you into your cage right now." She looked at Derek and said, "This has been a tiring morning for her. But tomorrow you can come over and help me clean her cage and feed her. Maybe I can teach her to say your name," she offered.

"Super," said Derek, not remembering until the words were out of his mouth that he had promised Rory he would never, ever speak to Bolivia.

Only two people kept back from the crowd around the bird. Rory wasn't going to give Bolivia the satisfaction of knowing how curious he was. And Edna was sitting on the ground stuffing herself with the grapes, banana, and apple that had been bait for the parrot. The fruit, thought Rory, had been superfluous. Just like Bolivia.

5
Twins or Triplets?

It was noon. The whole morning had been wasted, thought Rory with disgust. Mr. Dunn went off to school late, but still pleased with himself. Mrs. Dunn took Edna, who wasn't hungry now, into the house to have lunch. Derek and Rory went to get their sandwiches from the baskets of their bikes, which were lying where they had dropped them ages ago. They were lucky that the bicycles were in one piece with all the people tramping about, including the firemen with their heavy boots.

The boys sat down under the Currys' maple tree to eat. Rory's sandwich was cheese, and the filling had become runny from lying in the sun. It stuck to the roof of his mouth as he chewed it and made him thirsty.

As if she were reading his mind, Mrs. Golding walked through the hedge with a pitcher of lemonade. It would have been a welcome sight had she not been followed by Bolivia holding a fat sandwich that she obviously planned to eat sitting next to the boys.

Mrs. Golding poured the lemonade into paper cups she pulled from her apron pocket. "This has been some morning!" she exclaimed. "We certainly won't forget it for a long time."

"We've never had so much excitement around here before," said Derek, smiling.

Bolivia smiled back. Rory glared.

"It's going to be very hot today," said Mrs. Golding, "and you've all done an awful lot of running around after Lucette all morning. I'm going to treat the three of you to the movies this afternoon. How's that?"

"Great!" said Derek, not thinking again. "Rory and I were going to go swimming, but we can go swimming anytime."

"Not anytime," Rory disagreed. "We can't go when it rains."

"Well. Two against one want to go to the movies," said Bolivia. "We can go swimming tomorrow."

Derek looked to Rory for agreement.

Rory knew that the movie in town was one

that he and Derek had been wanting to see. But he didn't like the way Bolivia thought she could take over around here.

"I don't know if I want to go," he said.

"Then Derek and I will go without you," said Bolivia promptly.

Rory looked angrily at Derek.

"Come on, Rory," pleaded Derek. "You know we want to see this picture."

"Extra money for popcorn, of course," said Mrs. Golding. "What's a movie without popcorn, after all."

Rory wanted to say no. But what would he do all afternoon without Derek? Play in the sandbox with Edna? Besides, he thought, he'd better keep an eye on Bolivia before she got up to more tricks.

"How about soda?" he asked.

"Soda, ice cream, the works," said Mrs. Golding. "It's not every summer that my great-niece is here visiting me." She smiled at Bolivia.

So it was all arranged. Mrs. Golding went through the hedge to return her pitcher to her kitchen, and Bolivia followed her. "I'll meet you here in five minutes," she told the boys.

Rory was glad to have a few minutes alone with Derek. Derek was wearing a red-and-white striped shirt exactly like the one that

Rory was wearing. Their mothers often bought them matching shirts, knowing the boys liked to dress alike. Today even the red-and-blue stripes on their tube socks were matching. It was almost as if they were identical twins—except, of course, that they didn't look at all alike.

"Listen," said Rory. "There's something you should know. I was watching Bolivia this morning during all the fuss, and I'm pretty sure that Lucette didn't just accidentally escape from the house. I think Bolivia let her fly out. And she could have caught her anytime she wanted to if my father hadn't done it instead."

"You mean she planned it all?" asked Derek in amazement.

"Yes," said Rory, nodding his head.

"She's really something," said Derek with admiration. "Who knows what she'll think up next!"

"Oh, yeah? Well, we weren't even going to talk to her. What happened?" asked Rory. "I thought we were going to ignore her like she didn't exist."

"We'll ignore her another time," said Derek patiently. "Let's go to the movie today."

Just then Bolivia walked back through the hedge. Rory noticed immediately that she had changed her shirt. He didn't remember what she had been wearing before, but now she was wearing a red-and-white-striped one almost the same as his and Derek's.

"Look," she said, grinning at them. "Now we're triplets!"

Before they left for the movie, Rory ran into the house to tell his mother where they were going. He was tempted to change his shirt. On the other hand, he didn't want to leave Derek and Bolivia looking like twins.

As they walked along the hot street, Rory's anger grew inside him. Yesterday he and Derek had vowed they wouldn't speak to this girl and now they were all going to the movies together. Derek sold us out, he thought. He sold us out for a movie! Neither Derek nor Rory spoke, but Bolivia didn't seem to notice. She herself spoke constantly.

"Last winter I was in Vermont," she told them. "I saw the world's tallest snowman. His name was Abraham and he was over forty-seven feet tall."

"That's impossible," said Rory.

"No, it isn't," insisted Bolivia. "I saw it with my own eyes in St. Albans, Vermont. It was built by all the kids in the high school, and if you don't believe me you can read about it in the new edition of the *Guinness Book of Records* when it comes out."

"Sure, sure," said Rory in disbelief.

"Anyhow, it was built in February and didn't finish melting until May," said Bolivia. "But if it had been this hot in Vermont, he would have melted in one day."

"Wow!" said Derek. "I wish I could have seen it."

"Last summer I was in Israel. It never rains there in the summer," said Bolivia. "If someone says 'Let's go to the beach on Saturday' you never have to worry about whether it's going to rain."

"That's great," said Derek. "I wish it never rained here during our vacation."

"In Israel I went to the Dead Sea. It's so salty that nothing can live in it. No fish at all. That's why it's called the Dead Sea," said Bolivia.

Rory gritted his teeth. It was like walking down the street with a talking encyclopedia.

"You are giving us superfluous information," he said using the word he felt applied to Bolivia twenty-four hours a day.

Bolivia was quiet for a moment, but not longer.

"Where I live in Ithaca there is a famous bridge," she said.

"I'm a great swimmer," she said. "Wait till you see me. Can you dive?" she asked the boys. "I can dive off the high board and do a somersault."

Yeah, thought Rory, and probably sing the "Star Spangled Banner" on the way down.

Two women passed them on the street. "Isn't that sweet," said one. "They're wearing matching shirts. Are you related?" she asked them.

"Nope," said Derek. "Just good friends." It was the answer they always gave when they were questioned about wearing matching clothes. But there was no reason to include Bolivia in the answer. She wasn't their friend, Rory thought angrily.

As they neared the movie theater, Rory got an idea. "Let's get ice cream now instead of at the movie," he suggested. "They don't have many choices there—just chocolate and vanilla."

They stopped at the Carvel shop on the corner. "I want a soft chocolate cone," said Rory, when it was his turn.

"Hey, I thought you wanted something more interesting than chocolate," said Derek.

"I changed my mind," said Rory. Chocolate would work better for his plan.

As the three of them walked along, licking their cones, Rory tripped on something and his chocolate ice cream landed in the middle of Bolivia's shirt. "Ooops, sorry," he said, not feeling sorry at all.

In the movie, Rory just happened to spill a

cup of root beer on Bolivia's sleeve. And then holding a mushy chocolate bar, he accidentally walked into Bolivia as they were leaving the movie.

Bolivia might be wearing a red-and-white shirt, but it no longer matched his and Derek's, thought Rory with satisfaction. He didn't even mind that he had to sacrifice all his treats. He had been disappointed that all he could do was eat the container of popcorn. There was nothing to be gained by spilling it on Mrs. Golding's precious niece.

Bolivia's shirt was now covered with brown splotches of chocolate candy, ice cream, and soda.

"You're a mess," said Rory, inspecting her.

"Says who?" asked Bolivia. "The clumsiest kid in the world?"

Rory just laughed. He wondered if Bolivia would dare to copy the way he and Derek dressed in the future. She was a sharp one, no doubt about it. She knew what he was doing, but it happened too fast each time for her to avoid it. He would do it again if he had to. Maybe it would teach her to keep her distance.

"I wish I had a hot dog with lots of mustard," he said, looking Bolivia straight in the eye.

"I bet you do," she said.

"Yeah. You must be starved," said Derek. "You've spilled just about everything you had to eat this afternoon."

It was just like Derek to think all the spills were accidents, thought Rory.

"I'm getting a Coke," said Bolivia. "I have just enough money for one." She stopped at the open window of the candy store they were passing.

"Will you give us a drink?" asked Derek as Bolivia took the cup of soda.

"Ooops, sorry. I guess I can't give you any, Derek," said Bolivia, pouring the whole cup over Rory's head as she spoke. It dripped off his hair, onto his glasses, and his red-and-white shirt. The shirt was no longer clean. It looked like the one Bolivia was wearing.

"Boy. The two of you are really slobs," said Derek.

6

A Cold Day in July

Bolivia was everywhere. It was impossible for Rory to avoid her. She was standing outside his house when he opened the door in the morning. Sometimes she was even inside his house waiting for him. Rory's plan to ignore Bolivia had been abandoned and he had yet to come up with another scheme.

At first Rory had hoped that bike riding would be a way of escaping from her. But Derek's mother had taken her old bike out of the garage, and Mr. Golding had lowered the seat to fit Bolivia. The next thing Rory knew, Bolivia was pedaling beside them. And Mrs. Golding had gotten a membership in the pool so that Bolivia could go swimming with the boys.

Rory's sister Edna loved Bolivia. To prove it, she had renamed *all* of her dolls Bolivia. There was always a Bolivia underfoot in the

Dunn house. Rory liked to kick them and pretend they were the real thing.

The worst thing was that Derek liked Bolivia. "She's not so bad for a girl," he always said when Rory complained about her. "She grows on you."

"Yeah. Like poison ivy," said Rory. He remembered an expression that his grandmother often used when something seemed unlikely. "It will be a cold day in July before I get to like Bolivia," Rory told Derek. And as if to prove his words, it was the hottest July on record.

On the eighth day in a row of temperatures over ninety degrees, Derek and Rory and Bolivia were sitting in Derek's bedroom. They would have been at the pool, but Derek was being punished for not cleaning up his room. His bedroom looked like it had been hit by a tornado, his mother had said that morning when she told him he couldn't leave the house until he had sorted out the mess, picked up any of his things that were downstairs, and, for good measure, loaded the dishwasher.

"Your room doesn't look so bad," said Bolivia. "It just looks lived in."

"I feel like I'm melting," said Rory.

"It gets much hotter than this in Israel," said Bolivia, grabbing an armload of clothing from the floor and going to put it in the laundry hamper in the bathroom.

No matter what you said, she could top it, thought Rory. That was one of the things he hated most about her.

"So what if it's hot someplace else," he shouted after her. "I'm right here and I'm hot here."

There was a pile of clean laundry waiting on Derek's chest of drawers to be put away. Bolivia opened the drawers and stuffed as much as she could inside.

"You own too many shirts," she complained. "These don't fit in the drawer."

"Just put them back in the laundry," said Derek. "That's what I do. It's easier than putting them away."

"Let's think about winter," said Rory, sitting down on the floor. He was wearing nothing but a pair of cut-off jeans and the carpet itched him all over.

"Remember when we had twelve inches of snow last year and school was closed?" asked Derek, glad of an excuse to stop his cleanup.

Rory closed his eyes. "Remember, I could only find one of my boots, so I had to put on my father's and it kept falling off," he said, smiling.

"In Ithaca we usually get twenty inches of snow at a time," Bolivia informed them.

"Who cares?" said Rory. Bolivia had made him lose the cooling memory of last winter.

"I wish it would snow right now," said Derek.

"In the middle of a July heat wave? Fat chance," said Rory.

Derek's room looked better than before, now that the laundry, clean and dirty, had been disposed of, and the comics and games put away. "I'm supposed to vacuum it," sighed Derek, "but I'm too hot. Maybe my mother won't notice."

"Let's finish up downstairs," said Bolivia. It was possible she'd developed an immunity to hot weather with all her travels, thought Rory. She certainly had more energy than either he or Derek.

The boys reluctantly followed her downstairs. It was just as hot in the kitchen even though their teacher had taught them that hot air rises.

Bolivia began putting the dishes that were on the table into the dishwasher.

"It's awfully full," she said, as she tried to find a space for one of the cereal bowls.

Derek helped her move the dishes around so that everything would fit inside. "I guess I better turn it on or there won't be any clean dishes for supper," said Derek.

"Here. Use this," said Rory, holding out a bottle that was under the sink.

"I never saw my mother use that in the dishwasher," said Derek. "There should be a box of powder."

"Oh, come on, already," said Rory, impatiently squirting the yellow liquid into the machine. "This is wasting a whole day."

Derek closed the dishwasher and pushed the button to turn it on.

"Now what?" asked Bolivia.

"Let's have a snowball fight," said Derek, making a joke.

"I'd love a snowball fight more than anything else in the world," said Rory.

"We don't exactly have snow, but we do have something white and fluffy," said Bolivia.

"What?" asked Rory.

"Look," said Bolivia, pointing to the floor around the dishwasher. White suds were coming out the top and sides of the machine and flowing over the floor.

"Stop the machine!" Derek shouted.

Rory opened the door and the machine automatically stopped. But the suds did not. They continued to spill out onto the floor.

"I never saw that happen before," said Derek. "It must be broken."

"Maybe you shouldn't have used that liquid soap," said Bolivia.

"Why not?" asked Rory, remembering that he had been the one to pour the liquid into the machine. He reached for the bottle. It said Dishwashing Liquid with Extra Cleaning Power. "See. It's okay," he said, showing them.

"Some cleaning power," said Derek. "Help me with the floor."

The floor was covered with suds. Derek removed his sneakers and Bolivia and Rory did the same. The hot, sudsy water squished under their toes.

"What a way to wash your feet," said Rory.

"You said you wanted white," Bolivia reminded him as she grabbed a fistful of paper towels and tried to mop up some of the mess.

"What should we do with that?" asked Derek, pointing to the machine full of soap-suds and dishes.

"I think we should just let the wash cycle continue," said Rory. "Then it will all get rinsed away." Even if they were to take all the dishes out and wash them by hand, they would still have a machine full of soapy water to get rid of, so they decided to follow his advice.

Derek closed the diswasher and pushed the

start button again. It began to wash normally, but the suds soon slid down the side of the machine and onto the floor again. As quickly as they mopped it up, there were more white suds on the kitchen floor.

"My mother isn't going to like this," said Derek.

"Why not?" asked Bolivia as she mopped. "Besides clean dishes, she is going to have the cleanest kitchen floor for miles around."

Finally, the machine finished washing the dishes, and no more soapy water came out of it. Derek, Rory, and Bolivia finished mopping up the floor. It did indeed look shiny.

They stepped back to admire their handiwork. The garbage pail was filled with wet paper towels, but otherwise there was no sign that anything unusual had happened.

"You know what?" said Rory. "Now I'm hotter than ever."

"How about some ice cream?" offered Derek. "We've got half a gallon of vanilla in the freezer."

He reached for bowls and spoons and the ice-cream scoop. It took a minute for the ice cream to soften enough for Derek to dig out the first portion.

"That looks like a real snowball," said Rory.

"You're right," said Derek, admiring the ball of ice cream.

"I've got an idea!" said Bolivia.

"What?" asked Rory.

"Do you really want a snowball fight?"

"You can't have a snowball fight in July," said Rory.

"Yes, we can," said Bolivia. She snatched the scoop of ice cream out of the dish. "The question is, who should I throw this at?"

"Hey. Not in the kitchen," warned Derek. "We just cleaned this place up."

"No problem," said Bolivia, licking her fingers. "Bring that package and the scoop into the yard."

"You're crazy," said Rory. But he grabbed for the scoop. If Bolivia was going to throw a ball of ice cream at him, he was going to be ready to fight back.

The first ball of ice cream, already quite soft from the heat, hit Rory on the chin.

"You couldn't hit a brick wall," he shouted, licking his bottom lip and scooping a ball of ice cream to return the shot.

Bolivia saw the ball coming. She caught it in her right hand and took a lick before she threw it at Derek.

In no time, there were many white balls flying through the air. Some they caught and licked before they let them go. Others they missed. Some of the ice cream got into their mouths. Some landed on their shoulders and legs and some melted into dirty puddles on the ground.

Bolivia's red hair was soaking wet from melted ice cream. But unlike some girls who ran away from snowball fights right when it was the most fun, or worse yet, began to cry, Bolivia just laughed and laughed.

Half a gallon of ice cream doesn't last long when it is used for snowballs, but it was fun while it lasted. When it was all gone, the three children sat on the ground to catch their breath.

"That was fun," said Derek, licking his fingers.

"Boy, am I sticky," said Rory, licking his fingers, too.

"That's one way to clean off, but I've got a better idea," said Bolivia.

She went around the side of the house and came back with the garden hose. She turned it on Rory and Derek. Rory grabbed the hose and squirted her with the cold water. After all, she was sticky and needed washing off as well. While they were at it, they sprayed water in the yard to clean up the patches of melting ice cream.

Mrs. Golding opened her back door and called to her niece, "Bolivia, I need you for a couple of minutes."

Bolivia started off. "Wait till she sees me."

She giggled. "I'll be right back," she promised as she went through the hedge to her aunt's house.

Neither Rory nor Derek moved. It felt good to lie on the damp grass. They were both comfortably wet and cool after their game and sprinkling.

"That Bolivia is really terrific," said Derek. "Who'd ever think of a snowball fight in July? I don't even care if my mother has a fit when she discovers that the ice cream is all gone. It was worth it."

"It was okay," said Rory reluctantly.

"Okay? It was great," said Derek. "I wouldn't have even thought about going away if I had known how much fun she would be."

"What are you talking about?" asked Rory, sitting up. "Going away?"

"Oh," said Derek sheepishly. "You know how my mother's been talking about camp all spring and what a good experience it would be."

"Yeah. And we decided not to go," said Rory.

"You decided and I decided," said Derek. "But my parents decided that I had to go. They talked me into it."

"You mean you're going off to camp after all?" asked Rory. He couldn't believe that his friend would do a thing like that. "And you didn't even tell me," said Rory angrily.

"I just did tell you," said Derek, defending himself. "Besides, it's only for a couple of weeks. I'll check it out for us. If it's any good, we can go next summer together."

Rory felt absolutely betrayed. "I thought you were my best friend. I thought we never did things apart?"

"Yeah. Well, you had a chance to go to camp and you didn't want to go. Anyway, it isn't as if Bolivia wasn't here. You'll have a good time with her," promised Derek.

"I hate Bolivia," said Rory. "I hated her from the moment I heard about her and I still hate her. Everywhere we go, there she is. We don't have a second alone without her hanging around. She thinks she can do everything we do and go everywhere we go. I wish she had never come here."

"That's stupid," said Derek. "She's here and she's a lot of fun. You just won't admit that you're wrong. You just want everything to be your way all the time. Well, this time you can't have things your way." He paused to catch his breath. "I'm glad I'm going to camp. At least you can't boss me around while I'm there."

Derek jumped up and dashed into his house. The door banged shut behind him.

Rory stood on the grass. Water dripped off his hair and trickled down his glasses and his neck, but he hardly noticed. He was furious at Derek. "I'm glad he's going off to camp," he murmured to himself. "He can't talk to me like that and still be my friend."

"Hi!" shouted Bolivia, coming through the hedge. "I'm back."

But Rory tore past her and pushed through the hedge toward his own house.

7

At War with Bolivia

Darn propinquity! It was all well and good when Rory and Derek were best friends. But now that they had fought, it was hard to avoid someone who lived only two houses away.

"I have a headache," said Rory when his mother asked why he wasn't playing outside with his friends.

Friends! He hated them both!

Rory vowed never to speak to Derek again. He would ignore him, and he would ignore Bolivia, too. So he spent the rest of that hot afternoon inside the house pretending to be sick.

The next morning, Derek and Bolivia came knocking at the door. "Don't you want to go swimming?" they asked.

"No," said Rory. He slammed the door in their faces.

Derek and Bolivia knocked again.

"What do you want now?" asked Rory, opening the door a crack. "I said I don't want to go swimming."

"We could do something else," suggested Derek, as if he had forgotten the mean things he had said to Rory the day before.

"What would you like to do instead?" asked Bolivia.

"Nothing with you two!" said Rory angrily, and he slammed the door for a second time. Even if Derek had forgotten the fight, Rory remembered it.

They knocked again. But this time Rory didn't open the door. He went upstairs and from the window on the landing he watched them as they walked away, shrugging their shoulders.

Rory was angry at Derek and he didn't want to play with Bolivia. But seeing them go off together made him feel even worse. "There are other people I can be friends with," he told himself. He thought about riding over to Maurice's, but the idea didn't really appeal to him. So he just spent the day moping around the house.

"Is everything all right?" asked Mrs. Dunn.

"Yes," said Rory, though of course everything was all wrong. It was just about the longest day of his whole life.

The next morning no one came knocking at Rory's door. Rory thought they must have given up on him. But then his mother said, "Mrs. Curry is taking Derek shopping today to get all the things he needs for camp. Are you sorry that you aren't going to camp, too?"

"Not me," said Rory. "I don't want to go to any stinking old camp."

"What's camp?" asked Edna.

"It's a place where they tell you what to do all day and make you eat bad food and tell you when you have to go to bed," said Rory.

"That's just like home," said Edna.

"Wait a minute," said Mrs. Dunn. "I don't give you bad food."

"Last night you made me eat lima beans," said Edna.

"Camp is worse than home," said Rory. "They probably give you lima beans for breakfast."

"I don't want to go to camp," said Edna.

"Now see what you did," said Mrs. Dunn. "You're teaching Edna all your negative views of things."

"It saves her the trouble of finding out for herself," said Rory.

"How come you don't like camp?" Edna asked her brother, "You like lima beans."

After Derek's mother took him shopping,

she took him to the doctor to get a medical form filled out for the camp. So even though Rory walked around in his yard and rode his bike around the block a few times, he never saw Derek that entire day. He didn't see Bolivia either, but he wasn't looking for her. The Goldings had gone to visit friends and taken Bolivia with them.

There was only one more day before Derek left for camp. Rory wondered if his former friend would come over and apologize before he went away.

Just in case, Rory stayed around the house the next day. He didn't go to the pool with his family, he just stayed in the yard waiting for Derek. He wasn't going to forgive him, but he wanted to give his old friend a chance to set things right before he departed. It was another long day. Every day since Rory and Derek had fought seemed very long. Rory practiced shooting baskets, and he got several good shots. He was getting pretty good considering how short he was. He wished Derek could see. Then he got on his bike and rode around the block. There was no sign of either Derek or Bolivia. They're probably both off having a good time without me, he thought. So what? I don't need them.

And then it was Sunday and Derek was

gone. He had left without talking to Rory for two days and now he would be gone for two whole weeks. Good, thought Rory. I don't need him and now he won't be around to bother me.

Bolivia, however, was still around.

"Hi," she said, coming into Rory's yard. "What would you like to do today?"

"Nothing with you," said Rory. "Just leave me alone." He looked at her standing in front of him and grinning. It was her fault that he had had the fight with Derek. They had never had a fight before in all the years they knew each other.

"You're going to get awfully bored with Derek gone," she said. "We could do anything you want."

"Thanks, but no thanks," said Rory, turning back to the comic book he was reading. He had probably read it two dozen times before, but it was still more interesting than Bolivia.

"You creep," said Bolivia.

"It takes one to know one," said Rory, without looking up.

Bolivia left Rory, but she didn't go back home. Instead, she went into Rory's house and played with Edna. After a while, Mrs. Dunn came outside.

"I'm driving over to the pool with Edna and Bolivia. Are you coming with us?" she asked.

"No," said Rory.

"No, thanks," corrected his mother.

Rory didn't respond. He was too busy thinking of what he should do instead. He decided to pay a visit to Maurice. He hadn't seen him since the day in early July when he and Derek had gone to Maurice's house to hide from Bolivia. He didn't phone first. He never phoned Maurice. He just showed up at his door from time to time when it was convenient, like last winter when Derek had strep throat or when there was nothing else to do.

This time, there was no one home at Maurice's. Rory sat on the front step of Maurice's porch resting and trying to decide what to do next. He was thirsty from his bike ride, and he was annoyed that not only was Maurice not home, but neither was his mother, who might have offered him a cold drink before he went on his way. Now the question was, where should he go? It seemed silly to go back home when he had just come from there.

Rory considered joining his mother at the pool. He could swim in his shorts and get a ride home by putting the bike in the car trunk. But that would mean spending the afternoon with Bolivia. There was no way he wanted to do that.

He decided to ride over to the library. Maybe they were showing a movie this afternoon. He mounted his bike and set off. He had forgotten that it was Sunday. The library was closed. In disgust, he turned the bike around and slowly pedaled home along the hot streets.

At home he walked from his bedroom to the living room to the kitchen to the backyard and back to his bedroom again. There was nothing to do by himself. On one of Rory's rounds Mr. Dunn looked up from his typewriter, where he was doing work for school.

"Looking for something to do?" he asked Rory.

"Yeah," said Rory. "Could we do something together, like play Monopoly or something?"

"Not now," said Mr. Dunn. "This has to be finished by Tuesday. But the garden sure could use some weeding. How about it?" Rory walked to the window and looked out at the vegetables growing along the side of the house. Weeding was not his idea of how to pass an afternoon, but he couldn't think of an alternative, and so in the end he went out to do it. As he worked, he could hear Lucette's occasional squawks coming from inside the Goldings' house. She was probably bored, too.

Rory was so bored with the weeding that he was almost happy when his mother and the girls returned home. Edna's bikini was falling off as she got out of the car holding Bolivia's hand.

"Edna is going to visit Lucette," Bolivia called to Rory. "Do you want to come?"

"No," said Rory.

"No, thanks," said his mother.

"She doesn't want to go see Lucette either," said Rory, looking from his mother to Bolivia.

Actually, Rory really did want to see Lucette. More than he could ever admit to Bolivia, he enjoyed the time he and Derek had spent watching the parrot and listening to Bolivia speak with her. The summer before, when Bolivia had gone to Israel, Lucette had stayed behind with some friends and had not spoken a single word the entire time Bolivia was away. This summer, to make up for it, the bird spoke constantly and Rory laughed to hear words come out of the parrot's mouth.

But this time Rory pretended indifference even though it meant he had to continue weeding. In a little while, Bolivia and Edna came back.

"Bolivia is having supper at our house," said Edna. "She's going to sit next to me."

Rory shrugged. He wasn't surprised. Bolivia had won over his whole family except him. He'd just have to live with having her around. But it didn't mean that she was going to be his friend.

"Did you ever sell lemonade?" Bolivia asked at supper. They were drinking lemonade at the time, which was probably why she thought of it.

"Nope," said Rory. "Why bother?"

"It's a good way to earn money," said Bolivia. "I always wanted to do it, but I never lived anywhere in the summer where I could."

"I don't need any money," said Rory. "I get an allowance every week."

"It wouldn't be a bad idea to try and earn some money," suggested Mr. Dunn. "You won't get an allowance forever."

"I'll contribute half a dozen lemons and some sugar to get you started," offered Mrs. Dunn.

"Who said I wanted to sell lemonade?"

asked Rory. He wasn't going to be roped into something just because Bolivia wanted to do it.

"You know," said Bolivia. "You never want to do anything unless it's your idea. You're lucky that Derek goes along with you most of the time. I'm going to sell lemonade and if you don't want to do it with me, then I'll go into partnership with Edna."

"I love lemonade," said Edna, taking a big gulp from her glass.

"Edna can't even count over ten; how can she sell lemonade?" asked Rory.

"I can so count," said Edna indignantly. "I can count over a million." And she began, "A million and one, a million and two, a million and three. . . ."

It was pouring rain the next morning when Rory woke up, so the lemonade project was forgotten. Bolivia came over to his house and played with Edna. "I wish I had a little sister," she said to Rory. "You really are lucky."

After a while, when Edna was busy playing with all her Bolivia dolls, the real Bolivia said to Rory, "Would you like to play a game of Monopoly?"

"No," said Rory automatically. A moment later he realized that he should have agreed. Bolivia was right. Who else would play with him over the next two weeks? His parents were always too busy and his sister was too young.

"Too bad," said Bolivia. "I really feel like playing."

"Well, all right," said Rory. "I'll do you a favor and play with you this time." And he rushed to get the box with the game.

Bolivia stayed for lunch, but Mrs. Golding walked over, dripping rain from her umbrella into the house, to deliver a platter of freshly baked cookies. "When I invited Bolivia to spend the summer with us, I didn't mean for her to spend all her time here," she apologized to Mrs. Dunn.

"Don't be silly," said Rory's mother. "She's welcome to spend as much time here as she wants."

"I want a cookie," shouted Edna. "I could count a million cookies," she told Mrs. Golding. "A million and one, a million and two, a million and three. . . ."

8
Aurora Borealis

The days passed slowly. Gradually, out of boredom and desperation, Rory found himself spending more and more time with Bolivia. Mornings they went to the pool together and afternoons they played Monopoly or Clue or one of the other board games that Rory had amassed over several birthdays and Christmases. And gradually, too, he was forced to admit to himself that she wasn't so bad. He actually had a good time with her. Derek had been right. She wasn't bad for a girl. He wished that Derek were around so he could tell him. And he wondered if Derek would even talk to him when he returned home.

On the Monday after Derek had been gone for a week, both Bolivia and Rory received postcards from him. The cards had been addressed in Mrs. Curry's handwriting, Rory noticed quickly. She probably packed them into Derek's suitcase when he went away. Still, Derek didn't have to mail it, and so Rory was pleased to get it. The message read: Camp is fun. There are nice guys in my bunk, but you are still my best friend.

"Yahooo!" shouted Rory with delight. He rarely got any mail and certainly he had never received a postcard that made him this happy.

Bolivia showed Rory her card. It said: Camp is fun. There are nice guys in my bunk, but I miss you and Rory.

Rory grinned. "He'll be home in another week," he said. "We'll have to think of some good things to do together."

Bolivia nodded her head. "Look at this," she said, showing Rory another piece of mail that she had received. It was a letter from her parents. There were three large and colorful stamps on the envelope. "I know a kid who collects stamps," said Rory, thinking of Maurice. "If you don't want those, could I have them for him?"

"Sure," said Bolivia, tearing the corner off the envelope. She opened her letter and asked Rory if he had ever seen aurora borealis.

"Who's she?" asked Rory. "Is she on television?" The name sounded like someone famous from TV or the movies.

"Aurora borealis isn't a person. It's a thing," said Bolivia. "They are the northern lights, and you can sometimes see them in the sky during the summer. My father showed them to me a couple of years ago, and he wrote about it in this letter."

"I've only been in four states," Rory reminded Bolivia. "New Jersey, New York, Pennsylvania, and Connecticut. You're the big traveler around here. How could I have seen aurora borealis?"

"We might be able to see them right here in New Jersey if we're lucky," Bolivia explained. "We just need a clear night without clouds. Let's get my aunt and uncle and your parents to let us stay up very late. Then we'll go out and watch the sky." She thought a moment. "Did you ever sleep out in your backyard overnight?"

"No," said Rory. "Once before Edna was born we went on a camping trip, and I slept outside then."

"Let's sleep outside tonight," said Bolivia.

So that evening, way past their usual bedtime, Bolivia and Rory took the old blankets that Mrs. Dunn saved for trips to the beach out to the backyard. They walked about until they found a spot in the Goldings' yard where their vision wasn't blocked by trees or hedges.

It felt strange to Rory to be lying on his back in the yard in the middle of the night looking up at the stars, and all because Bolivia had received a letter from her father halfway around the world.

He squinted upward, trying to be the first to see a shooting star or this thing called aurora borealis. He liked the sound of its name. Aurora borealis. Aurora borealis. It had a nicer ring to it than any of the special words his father had ever taught him.

"Stars are so far away, it's hard to imagine what they are really like," he said to Bolivia. After he spoke, he wondered why he had. She would probably laugh at him, he thought, angry at himself. If Derek had been here, he would have understood.

"Each one is really a sun that is billions and billions of miles away from us," said Bolivia.

Rory thought of Edna. He could imagine her counting out, "a billion and one, a billion and two. . . ."

"The stars make me feel as tiny as an ant or a beetle," Bolivia said. "It's just like archeology."

"How can that be?" Rory asked. "Archeology studies old things. Astronomy is about outer space."

"I know. But my father says they are both ways of digging into things," explained Bolivia. "Archeologists dig deeper and deeper into the earth, and the deeper they go, the more they learn about ancient times. The more they learn, the smaller man seems in relation to the universe."

Rory nodded in the dark with understanding. "Astronomers search deeper and deeper into space," he said. "Do you ever wonder about whether there are people up there like us?"

"Sure," Bolivia said.

Rory realized that she was whispering, and he had been whispering, too. There was something about being out alone in the dark under the stars that made him want to speak softly. It was almost like being in church.

"I wonder what they are like?" he asked.

"Maybe they are lying in the dark, looking out toward us just now and wondering, too," mused Bolivia.

"In the nighttime, in the dark," said Rory, "none of the things that are important during the day, like Little League games and school, seem to matter very much."

"I know what you mean," said Bolivia. "If I

wake up in the night, I think about my parents."

"Do you miss them?" asked Rory. He had never been away from home for more than three nights, and that was once when he went to Hershey, Pennsylvania, with Derek and his parents.

"It's funny," said Bolivia. "I didn't want to go to Turkey this summer. I wanted a regular summer like other kids. Then when they arranged for me to stay here in Woodside instead of going to Turkey, I got angry. I thought they were just getting rid of me."

"But you didn't want to go to Turkey," said Rory.

"I know. I guess I didn't know what I wanted. It's funny," said Bolivia. "During the day I hardly think about my parents. But at night I always do. They seem so much farther away in the dark."

"But it's the same distance," Rory pointed out.

"I know," said Bolivia. "And I love Woodside. I'm glad I'm here."

"Isn't Woodside boring compared with all those faraway places that you've been to?" asked Rory.

"It's not boring, just different," said Bolivia. "I wish I had a little sister or brother, and I wish my parents weren't so involved

85

with ancient times and thought more about the present. That's why I love Woodside. Everyone here is thinking about right now."

"Well, you're lucky not to have a little sister," said Rory. "My parents used to spend a lot more time with me before Edna was born. Then once she was around they were so busy oohing and ahing that they didn't think about me anymore." Rory was surprised he had said that aloud. It was something he thought about a lot, but he had never mentioned it, not even to Derek.

"I'm glad we're friends, Rory," Bolivia said after awhile. "It makes me feel less lonely and less scared when I wake up in the middle of the night. And Rory, I think you're wrong about your parents. They just think you're older so you can be more independent. It's great the way you're allowed to get on your bike and go off riding anywhere you want."

In the dark, Rory blushed. He hadn't worked very hard at being Bolivia's friend, he thought, but maybe he was. Certainly he liked her better tonight than he had. She didn't seem so know-it-all in the dark, and he liked what she said about his being grown-up and independent.

"Look," said Bolivia, suddenly sitting up. "Over there." She pointed her finger. "Did you see it?"

"What? Where?" asked Rory. He had almost forgotten the reason that he and Bolivia were outside in the night.

"It was like a white light over beyond Derek's house. Watch. Maybe you'll see another one. It was a shooting star."

Rory lay straining his eyes toward the sky. He didn't want to miss this special sight. It was amazing how quiet the street was around them. Hardly any cars drove by at this hour, and almost all the lights were off in the houses. Except for an occasional cricket and the cicadas, there were no other sounds or signs of life.

It was so quiet that he could even hear Bolivia's breathing beside him. Neither of them said anything more. They just lay looking up overhead waiting for the next burst of light. Rory thought about what they had been saying. It was strange what you could say in the dark that you would never admit to in the daylight.

A plane droned by overhead in the distance. Rory wondered if it were taking someone to Turkey or some other place far away. He was going to ask Bolivia, but somehow the quiet was so nice that he didn't want to break into it. So instead he listened as the plane moved farther and farther away until he could hear it no longer.

Suddenly Rory saw a flash of light in the sky. "Look," he said, sitting up excitedly. "I see a shooting star!"

Bolivia didn't respond. She had fallen asleep.

So Rory, hypnotized, watched the space where the momentary flash had occurred. There was no word that his father had taught him that could describe the wonder of it.

He lay back on the ground watching and hoping to see the lights of the aurora borealis. How wonderful that would be.

But like Bolivia, Rory didn't see the northern lights. He fell asleep in the quiet midsummer strangeness of the backyard, next to his friend.

9
The Lemon-Aid Business

"**O**KAY. Today's the day," Bolivia announced two mornings later when she appeared at Rory's door. "It's hot and we've got nothing to do. So today I'm opening my lemonade stand. Are you with me or not?"

If he could have thought of a single alternative, Rory might have said no. But it no longer seemed important to disagree with everything Bolivia said. Rory shrugged his shoulders. "I suppose so," he said.

"Get some paper and make a sign," instructed Bolivia. "I'll go get some supplies from my aunt."

Bolivia was gone before Rory could protest.

So he located some construction paper and a red marker. In big letters he wrote Lemon-Aid 15¢. Bolivia hadn't said anything about the price, but he felt that if he was making the sign, he had the right to make that decision.

Mr. Golding helped Bolivia bring an old card table out to the curb. Mrs. Golding contributed a large plastic pitcher and a bucket of ice cubes. "I'll give you more when those are melted," she promised. Mrs. Dunn donated the lemons and the sugar that she had offered. She showed Rory how to squeeze the lemons with a small juicer.

Edna came outside to watch. "I want some lemonade," she said.

"It costs fifteen cents," said Rory, pointing to his sign, even though Edna didn't know how to read.

"I want some lemonade," Edna whined again.

"Let her have a little cup," said Bolivia. "After all, your mother supplied all the lemons and the sugar."

Rory poured a small amount of the lemonade into a paper cup. The cup had clowns and a circus motif on it. It was one of a package of cups that was left over from Edna's birthday party in May when she had turned three.

"More," demanded Edna as soon as she finished gulping down her drink.

"No more," said Rory. "This is a business. We can't give away all of our product."

"More," said Edna.

"Later," said Bolivia, smiling at the little girl. "We'll give you more later."

That answer satisfied her, and Edna went off into the yard to play on the gym set. Rory looked up and down the street watching for their first paying customer. There was no one in sight.

"Keep cool," said Bolivia. "We haven't even been out here ten minutes."

But twenty minutes passed and still there were no customers in sight. "Maybe you should bring Lucette outside. You could even set her free. If the fire department comes we're sure to get a big crowd."

Bolivia shook her head. "I don't want her to get overexcited," she said.

"You didn't worry that other time," Rory pressed on, annoyed. It was boring sitting and waiting for customers.

Just then, Mrs. Caspar, who lived on the next block, limped down the street with her French poodle. "Would you like to buy a cup of lemonade?" Bolivia called out to her. "It's very cooling and refreshing on a hot morning like this."

"Does it have sugar in it?" asked Mrs. Caspar.

"Sure. It's nice and sweet," said Rory.

"I'm on a sugar-free diet," Mrs. Caspar said.

So much for their first potential customer.

"What happened to your foot?" asked Bolivia.

"New shoes. I've gotten a terrible blister," said the woman.

"Would you like me to give Daniella her walk?" Bolivia offered. "You could go home and take off those shoes."

"What a thoughtful suggestion." Mrs. Caspar smiled. She gave the leash to Bolivia. The girl and the dog went off, and Mrs. Caspar turned around and limped toward the corner and her home.

"More lemonade," said Edna, returning.

"Not now," Rory said.

"It's later now," said Edna.

Rory was starting to feel thirsty himself. "I'll share a cup with you," he said, pouring out a full cup of the liquid from the pitcher. He took a long, thirsty gulp. It was good. "Here," he said, giving Edna the little bit left in the bottom of the cup.

She smiled at him anyway.

When Bolivia returned from walking the dog, she was thirsty, too. "Here," she said, putting a quarter in the little box that was to hold their profits. "Mrs. Caspar paid me this for walking Daniella. I guess I can buy a cup of lemonade with it."

Rory poured her a cup. "I can't give you any change," he said.

"That's okay," said Bolivia. She refilled her cup halfway. "I'll just take some more lemonade."

"I took a cup while you were gone," Rory admitted, and looked in his pocket for money to pay her. He didn't have anything.

"Pay me later," said Bolivia.

The pitcher was half-empty and the ice cubes were all melted, but still there were no other customers in sight.

"I've never seen this street so empty," said Rory.

"Maybe I should let Lucette out," said Bolivia.

Mr. Dunn came out of the house.

"Do you want to buy a cup of lemonade, Dad?" asked Rory.

"No, thanks. I've just had a glass of orange juice inside. I've got to wash the car. It looks awful." He thought a moment. "Could you kids give me a hand? I'll move the car right near your lemonade stand, and you can wash the car and sell lemonade at the same time."

"Sure," said Bolivia. "Why not?"

"Just don't wash the car with lemonade." Mr. Dunn laughed. He went inside to get a pail of water and a couple of sponges. Then he backed the car onto the street in front of the card table.

"Hey. You spelled the sign wrong," he said.

Rory blushed. He was good at remembering the big words that his father taught him, but he was not good at spelling them. When you said a word, no one ever knew if you could spell it or not.

Rory shrugged as he squeezed out the sponge. "It doesn't matter," he said. "Nobody's been around to read it anyhow."

Mr. Dunn brought the vacuum cleaner and an extension cord outside. "Would you please clean the inside of the car, too?"he asked Rory. "Edna was eating cookies in there, and the back seat looks like an apple-crumb pie without the apples."

Rory sighed. If he'd gone to the pool instead of giving in to Bolivia and selling lemonade, he wouldn't have to spend the morning doing chores. As he moved the vacuum hose around inside the car, he noticed something shiny on the floor. It was a dime. He looked about in case there was any more money. He didn't want to vacuum it up. Sure enough, under the front seat he found two quarters and another dime.

"Hey, Dad," Rory called to his father. "Look what I found." He held out his hand to show off the seventy cents.

"Now, that's what I call serendipity!" said Mr. Dunn, smiling.

"What's that?" asked Rory.

"It's a new word for you," said Mr. Dunn. "Ser-en-dip-ity. It's when you find something that you weren't even looking for." He smiled at Rory and Bolivia. "The money must have fallen out of my pocket when I was driving. Keep it, and thanks for such a good job." He got into the clean car. "I'm off to school now," he said. "See you this evening."

"I'm going to buy another cup of lemonade," said Bolivia.

"Me, too," said Rory.

He put the seventy cents into the money box and poured out two drinks. The lemonade was no longer very cold, but it was still wet and sweet.

"I want more," said Edna, seeing them both drinking. "It's later again."

Bolivia drained the pitcher into Edna's cup.

"I'll go get some more ice and water from the house," she said.

When she came out, she brought a couple of sandwiches with her. "My aunt fixed us these for lunch," she said. "We don't want to have to go inside and lose business."

"What business?" asked Rory. But he grabbed one of the sandwiches. They were roast beef, his favorite.

Of course, the sandwiches made them thirsty. "My aunt offered to bring out a couple of glasses of milk for us," said Bolivia. "But I thought it would be bad advertising for us to be drinking milk and selling lemonade at the same time."

"Selling?" asked Rory. "Who to? Listen," he said. "I'm going to drink another cup of lemonade with my sandwich."

"Me, too," said Bolivia. "That's good advertising."

Mrs. Dunn came out of the house to see how they were doing. "Do you want some lemonade?" asked Bolivia.

"To tell the truth, I prefer iced tea in the summer," said Rory's mother. She took Edna by the hand and the two of them went inside for lunch.

"Maybe we should sell iced tea," said Bolivia.

"I don't like iced tea," said Rory, pouring himself another cup of lemonade. Bolivia took another cup, too.

A car drove by and slowed down in front of the card table. "I think we finally got a real customer," said Rory excitedly. The window of the car rolled down and a woman's head looked out.

"Do you want to buy a cup of lemonade?" asked Bolivia.

"Oh, no, thanks," said the woman. "I'm on my way to a luncheon. Isn't this Dogwood Lane?"

Rory shook his head. "That's on the other side of town," he explained. "People always confuse Dogleg with Dogwood." He counted off in his head. "You have to go three more blocks and make a left at the traffic light. Then all the streets are named after trees. Maple Lane, Cherry Lane, and Dogwood Lane."

"Thanks a lot," said the woman as she rolled her window up. The car moved down the street. Then, as they were still watching, the woman backed up the car and it came toward them again.

"Maybe she changed her mind," said Rory.

The car stopped in front of them and the window opened again. "The least I can do is pay for the directions if I'm not buying a drink," said the woman, and she stuck her hand out. Bolivia reached toward it and took the dime the woman offered.

"Thanks," she called out, as the car went off again.

There was now one dollar and five cents in the money box, and they still hadn't sold a single cup of lemonade except to themselves.

"This is getting boring," said Rory. "There's nothing to do but drink lemonade." As he said it, he poured himself another cup.

"No, it isn't," argued Bolivia. "You can't expect to open a lemonade stand and automatically have a line of customers waiting." She poured herself another drink also.

"I'll be right back," Rory told Bolivia, and he went into the house. After drinking so many cups of lemonade, he needed to use the bathroom.

When his mother saw him, she handed him several letters that she wanted mailed. "Can you just drop those in the box at the corner?" she asked.

Rory took the letters and told Bolivia that he would be right back. "If you see the mailman, ask him if he wants to buy a cup of lemonade," Bolivia called after him.

Rory didn't see anyone. But as he dropped the letters into the box, he did see something lying by the curb. It was an old, worn coin purse, and he picked it up with curiosity. He had never found anything like that before. He opened it and inside he could see several dollars and coins, too.

Rory ran back to the lemonade stand with the purse. "Look what I found," he said showing it to Bolivia. "This is a day for serendipity," he said, remembering the new word.

"Is there a name inside?" asked Bolivia.

Rory dumped the contents of the purse on the table. In all there was seventeen dollars and eighty-two cents, but there was no name or any other clue to who owned it. "If we can't find the owner, I can keep it," said Rory. This might be a profitable day after all.

"Listen, Rory," said Bolivia. "Seventeen dollars and eighty-two cents is a lot of money. We've got to make an effort to find the owner. It might be someone who needs that money."

"I know," said Rory reluctantly. It had only been a wish that he would be able to keep the money.

"Where did you find the purse?" asked Bolivia.

"Next to the mailbox."

"Then it probably belongs to someone right around here who lost it when he or she mailed a letter," she said.

"We can't go ringing every doorbell and asking people if they mailed a letter today," said Rory. "There are too many houses."

"Then at least we should make a sign and leave it on the mailbox." She tore a strip of paper off their lemon-aid sign. "Wait. I'll go and get a pencil," she said, running into her aunt's house.

Bolivia returned with a pen and a roll of tape. "We can't say what we found, because then anyone can say it's theirs," she explained. She thought a moment. *Did you lose something? Ask at the Lemon-Aid stand in front of 26 Dogleg Lane. If you know what it is, you will get it back.*

She ran down the street to post the little notice on the mailbox.

"Now we have to wait and see what happens," she said when she returned.

Ten minutes after Bolivia had put up the sign, two teen-age boys came by. "Hey, what did you find?" asked the first.

"None of your business," said Bolivia.

"I lost some money," said the second. "I had a hole in my pocket."

"How much?" asked Rory suspiciously.

"Five dollars?" asked the boy.

"Nope," said Bolivia.

"Ten dollars?" asked the boy.

"Nope," said Rory.

"Would you like to buy a cup of lemonade?" asked Bolivia.

"How can I?" asked the boy. "I don't have any money. Besides, it's probably sour."

"One dollar?" asked his friend.

It was obvious to Rory that neither of these boys had lost the little purse, and he was happy when they went off down the street.

A woman stopped at the stand as she walked by. "I saw your note," she said. "What did you find?"

"We can't tell," said Bolivia. "But if you lost it and can describe it, we'll give it back."

"No, I didn't lose anything. I was just curious," she said. And she walked on before they could even try to sell her a drink.

"Well, at least people are beginning to stop and talk to us," observed Bolivia. "That's progress."

She poured another cup of lemonade for herself and one for Rory. "We've finished up this pitcher. I'll go and get more ice and water," she said.

She came running out of the house without the ice or the water or the pitcher.

"Guess what?" she asked. "My aunt was just on the phone with her friend Mrs. Tillinghast. And she told my aunt that she lost her coin purse and she's afraid it may have been stolen. So I asked her to describe it, and she did, exactly. Except she thought there was about fifteen dollars inside."

"Should we take it to her?" offered Rory.

"No. She's on her way over here herself," said Bolivia. "She only lives two blocks away."

Within five minutes a car drove up and stopped in front of the house.

"That must be Mrs. Tillinghast," said Bolivia as an elderly woman stepped out and started coming toward them. She thanked both children many times and told them how relieved she was.

Rory took the coin purse out of the pocket of his jeans where he had put it for safekeeping. He felt a twinge of disappointment.

Mrs. Tillinghast opened the coin purse. She doesn't even trust us, thought Rory. Now she's going to count all her money to see if I took any. But instead, the old woman removed a five-dollar bill and put it down on the table. "I can't thank you both enough," she said, beaming at them.

"Oh," she said, looking at the sign. "A lemonade stand. I used to sell lemonade with my sister when we were little. I'd like to buy a cup, for old times' sake."

Rory reached for the pitcher to pour out a cup, but the pitcher was still inside the house where Bolivia had left it.

"Just a minute," said Bolivia, and she rushed inside for it. Rory reached under the table for the box with the lemons, but there were none left. "Just a moment," he said, and he rushed into his house to get a new supply.

Bolivia came out quickly, bringing the

pitcher filled with water and ice, but Rory returned without any lemons. He had used the last one his mother had.

"Would you like a cup of cold water?" Bolivia offered. "It's free."

Mrs. Tillinghast laughed. "Sure," she said and drank down the water.

When she left, Rory turned to Bolivia. "I think it's time to retire from the lemonade business. We finally had a real customer and we didn't even have any lemonade left to sell her."

"That's okay," said Bolivia. "Look at all the money we collected."

There was six dollars and five cents in the little box.

"That's incredible," said Rory. "We made all that money and we didn't sell a single cup—except to each other."

"You know what?" observed Bolivia. "You tell your father that you didn't make a mistake on that sign at all. We've been selling *aid* all day long. Lemon *aid*."

"Right!" said Rory, pleased with himself. "How shall we spend the profits?"

10
What Rory Dunn Did

E ven Bolivia, who rarely lacked for ideas,
couldn't think of something really special to buy with the six dollars and five cents
that they'd earned selling lemon-aid. "Let's
save it until we come up with a super plan,"
she said. It seemed sensible. They didn't want
to spend their earnings on ice cream or movies when those were things that they were
usually given money for anyhow. "Maybe
when Derek comes back he'll think of something we can all do with the money," said
Bolivia.

"That's not fair. He didn't earn any of it,"
pointed out Rory.

"I thought he was your best friend."

"I guess so," said Rory. Bolivia's ideas about
friendship were different from his.

The day after the lemon-aid business, she
came over to his house and said, "What do

you want to do today? I picked yesterday, so you should choose today."

Rory was surprised. He never did it that way with Derek. He usually told Derek what they were going to do. But he supposed she was right. It was fairer to take turns—especially when it was his turn.

Gradually, the days passed. Derek would be home in a couple of days, and Rory had to admit that he was having a good time with Bolivia. On the days when it was his turn to make the plans, they usually went to the pool. But on Bolivia's days, they did different things. Once she convinced her aunt to take them to a place where you could pick your own blueberries. It had been hot standing in the sun filling cardboard containers with the tiny berries. "Why don't we just buy some at the supermarket?" Rory wanted to know. "You can't eat them in the supermarket," Bolivia said, popping another berry into her mouth.

"Wait till you taste the pie I'm going to make when we get home," said Mrs. Golding. "Then you'll be glad that we came here." She smiled at her niece. "Imagine, here are berries growing twelve miles from where we live, and when we go to the store we buy berries that were shipped hundreds of miles from Oregon."

Mrs. Golding's pie was fantastic. As he was sitting in her kitchen and eating a large slice, Rory decided that berry picking had paid off after all. "I'd never picked berries before," Bolivia explained. "I want to do everything in the world."

The day before Derek returned home, Bolivia went shopping with her aunt. "You can come along," said Mrs. Golding. Rory shook his head. He would hate to spend a day walking through department stores. It was better to walk around with bare feet and do nothing.

"I want to buy clothes for Bolivia for when she goes back to school," said Mrs. Golding. "I've never had a daughter, and this is my big chance."

Rory thought about his mother with a daughter and a son. He didn't think she thought it was so wonderful to go shopping for new clothing for them. After Bolivia left with her aunt, Rory didn't know what to do with himself. He was used to doing things with Bolivia.

It looked like rain, so he couldn't go swimming. He remembered the stamps Bolivia had given him for Maurice and wondered if Maurice were around. But he didn't want to risk a long bike ride in the rain.

Rory took the basketball out of the garage

and dribbled it aimlessly for a bit. He threw the ball and made a couple of good foul shots. He was getting better and better. But it wasn't fun unless there was someone around to see how good he was.

Rory walked over to the Goldings' house. Mr. Golding was raking the leaves in his front yard. It was still August, but already some leaves were falling. Before long, autumn would be here and school would be starting again. Bolivia would be gone then, too. Rory realized that he would miss her. He would miss Lucette, too, he thought.

"Can I go upstairs and look at Lucette?" he asked Mr. Golding.

"Sure," said the old man. "You know the way, and the door's open."

Rory wiped his bare feet on the doormat and went inside the Golding house and up the stairs to the room that had been Bolivia's all summer.

"Hello there. Hello there," squawked Lucette.

Rory laughed. "Hello, yourself," he answered back.

"Hello there. Hello there," the bird repeated, glad to have an audience.

Rory felt in his pockets. He wished he had something with him to feed Lucette. He poked his fingers through the cage and stroked the bird's red-and-green feathers.

The bird enjoyed the attention. She rubbed up against Rory's hand. Sometimes, Bolivia opened the cage door and let Lucette walk up and down her arm. A few times the bird had even walked on Rory's arm or stood on his head. Bolivia had promised that before she went home she would get her uncle to take a picture of Rory and Derek each holding Lucette. That would be something to show off at school, he thought.

One thing that still annoyed Rory about Bolivia was that she never let either of the boys open the parrot's cage. She always had to be the one to do it. The catch on the door was very simple to open. Bolivia would never know if he opened it now and let Lucette walk on his arm. The bird was lonely and it would make her happy to have Rory let her out of the cage for a few minutes. Why not? he thought. Bolivia did it all the time. Why shouldn't he?

Rory slid the catch and the cage door swung open.

"Hello there," shrieked Lucette, and she flew out. Instead of climbing onto Rory's arm the way she always climbed onto Bolivia's, the bird flew to the top of the open closet door.

"Hey. Come on down," Rory called to the bird.

But the parrot would not listen to Rory. Suddenly Rory remembered the day that Lucette had flown out of the window. He rushed over to the window and saw that there was a screen on it. Well, now he knew for one hundred percent certain that Bolivia had let that bird out of the house. Looking out the window, he saw Mr. Golding putting the leaves that he had raked into a large plastic bag. Mr. Golding looked up and, seeing Rory, waved to him.

Rory wondered if Mr. Golding could see that Lucette was out of the cage. He turned around and tried again to catch the parrot. He had better put her back inside her cage before anyone knew what he had done. Rory pushed a chair over to the closet, but before he could even step onto it, Lucette flew out of the bedroom. He should have closed the door first thing. How could he have been so stupid?

The bird was now circling the other upstairs bedrooms. Rory followed Lucette into Mr. and Mrs. Golding's bedroom, but as soon as he entered, Lucette flew out again. Rory tripped over a leg of a chair, banging his foot, as he rushed out into the hallway

after Lucette. Somehow Rory felt that the parrot was laughing. She was having a good time.

Rory wondered if he should go downstairs and ask Mr. Golding to help him. He was embarrassed to tell his neighbor what he had done. He could say that the cage door opened by itself, but he didn't think he would believe him. The door had never opened by itself before.

Lucette flew into Bolivia's room again. Rory slammed the door before the bird could get out. Now the bird was safely inside the room, but Rory was outside it. How could he put her back inside the cage? He sat down on the floor outside the room and looked at the middle three toes of his right foot. He had really banged them, and they hurt badly. He could scarcely move them at all. When he tried to stand up again, he could hardly bear to put any weight on his right foot. He didn't know how he would ever manage to walk down the stairs and go home again.

He would just have to leave Lucette inside the room and wait for Bolivia to take care of her. He would have to admit what he had done. He wouldn't be surprised if Bolivia never spoke to him again.

Rory heard the front door slam. Mr. Golding had come into the house. He looked up to the top of the steps and saw Rory sitting there. "Hello," he called up to Rory.

"Hi," Rory called back softly. He felt like crying. His foot hurt worse and worse.

Mr. Golding climbed the stairs slowly. That was the way the old man always climbed the stairs, thought Rory.

"Why are you sitting on the floor?" asked Mr. Golding. "Don't you like my chairs?"

"I can't move my foot," Rory whispered. "And I let Lucette loose." Better to say it and get it all over with at once.

"What? Lucette hurt your foot?" asked Mr. Golding. He went to open the door of Bolivia's room.

"No. Don't open it!" shouted Rory. "Lucette is loose. She'll fly around the house if you open the door. Bolivia knows how to catch her. Wait till she comes home."

Mr. Golding nodded his head. "But how did she hurt your foot?" he asked. "She's very tame. Even when she eats from your hand, she never pecks at your finger."

"It's not her fault," said Rory. "I tripped on a chair."

Mr. Golding bent down and looked at Rory's foot. Even in the dim light of the hallway, it was easy to see that the foot was swollen. And the area around the toes was turning blue and purple.

113

Mr. Golding whistled under his breath. "I'm going to call your mother and then we'll call the doctor, too."

Mrs. Dunn came right over, followed by Edna. His mother's face looked strangely white, Rory thought.

"Now, don't worry," Mr. Golding was saying to her. "Nobody ever died of a broken foot."

"Can you make it downstairs?" asked Mrs. Dunn. The doctor had said to bring Rory over to his office.

Rory tried standing up. It was very painful.

"Can you do it like Edna does?" asked Mrs. Dunn. Edna had her own way of climbing down stairs. She sat on her bottom and slid down, one step at a time.

"Good idea," said Mr. Golding. So Rory slowly made his way down the stairs. It had always looked easy when Edna did it, but he had to be careful not to bump his right foot. Once his foot came down too hard and he actually saw stars, just like in comic books when someone gets punched and there's a burst of stars above his head. Edna thought it was funny to see her big brother bumping his way down.

It was probably the most stupid thing that had ever happened to him, Rory thought afterwards. At least if he had a big cast on his foot he could show it off to Bolivia and Derek. But although Rory had indeed broken two toes, the doctor said there was nothing to be done.

"You mean I'm not going to get a cast?" Rory had complained.

"Nope," said Dr. Maxwell, smiling. "A broken toe just needs time to heal itself. I must get a dozen cases each summer," he said.

"How about crutches?" asked Rory hopefully.

"No. Not necessary," said the doctor. He turned to Mrs. Dunn. "Just cut a hole in his old sneakers so that it won't hurt so much when he walks. But in three weeks or so, he'll be running around again like old times."

They drove home together, Mrs. Dunn and Rory sitting in the front seat, Mr. Golding and Edna sitting in the back. "You'll be better in no time," said Mr. Golding, snapping his fingers. Edna tried snapping her fingers.

"Like this," Mr. Golding said, and all the way home he helped Edna position her fingers and try to snap them.

By the time they arrived at 26 Dogleg Lane, Mrs. Golding and Bolivia were waiting for them.

Rory took a deep breath. He had to explain to Bolivia how Lucette had gotten out of the cage.

"Look what your dumb bird did to me," he said as he limped out of the car.

"How come you were playing with her?" Bolivia demanded. "You didn't have any right to open the cage."

"Oh, yeah? What right did you have to let her fly out the window and make such a fuss that your aunt had to call the fire department? You could have caught Lucette if you wanted to. It was a false alarm. You should have been arrested."

Once the words were out of his mouth, Rory was sorry. He didn't want to get Bolivia into trouble.

Bolivia just grinned. "Don't be angry." She laughed. "I put Lucette in her cage. It's okay." She looked at Rory. "Does your foot hurt very badly?"

Rory nodded his head. "I won't be able to run around very much or anything," he complained, hoping for some sympathy.

"It will be better in a snap," said Edna, quoting Mr. Golding.

She squeezed her little fingers together the way she had been taught, but there was no sound. Instead, from upstairs they could all hear a loud squawk. It was Lucette chuckling at the trouble she had caused.

11
The Great
Pizza Pig-Out

Rory sat on a lounge chair in his backyard, hurting in two places. His poor toes hurt him because he had forgotten and stepped down hard on them a few minutes ago. The other hurt was in the pit of his stomach. It wasn't a stomachache exactly. It was the queasy feeling he had before an arithmetic test. But that was silly because it was still summer vacation and Rory didn't have to worry about arithmetic tests for weeks. What he was worrying about was that Derek would be returning home in a few minutes. Rory had been thinking a lot about Derek. The boys hadn't even spoken to each other for two days before Derek left for camp. And even though Derek had sent him a postcard right at the beginning, perhaps he had changed his mind. Or maybe he had made so many new friends since then that he wouldn't need Rory anymore.

Rory moved his toes gingerly and thought about how it was before. Before the summer and before Bolivia. The two boys had so much fun together, and they had never argued about anything. Now he knew that Derek had been right. Bolivia was fun, too, even if she was a girl and had been foisted on them. He hadn't been very fair to her when she first came to Woodside. But how could he explain to Derek that he had changed his mind? Probably now that Derek was back, Bolivia would go bike riding or swimming with him and Rory would just have to sit still and rest his toes.

So Rory sat pretending to read the new comics that Mr. Golding had bought for him, but really he was listening for the Currys' car to drive up with Derek inside. He waited anxiously when he heard Derek's father pull into his driveway. The car doors opened and banged shut and Rory sat holding his breath. Would Derek come looking for him? Minutes passed. I was right, thought Rory sadly. He didn't come running right over. He doesn't want to be my friend anymore.

Fifteen minutes later, Derek came running

into the Dunn yard. He was tanned and taller than ever, and he was carrying his old comics. "I heard all about your foot," he said. "I thought you would want to borrow these."

Derek sat on the ground next to the lounge chair. "I can't stay long," he apologized. "My parents are taking me out to dinner. But tomorrow it will be like old times, being back home and doing things with you."

"I can't go to the pool or anything," said Rory sadly. "You'll probably want to go swimming."

"No," said Derek, shaking his head and standing up. "I haven't seen you in a long time. And, besides, I did plenty of swimming at camp."

The next day Derek and Bolivia and Rory spent most of the afternoon assembling a 500-piece puzzle on the bridge table that had served as their lemonade stand. Rory and Bolivia told Derek about their business venture.

"We made six dollars and five cents," said Rory proudly.

"And we didn't sell even a single cup of lemonade," said Bolivia.

"Except to each other," Rory reminded her. "And Edna."

"We still haven't come up with a good way

to spend the money," said Rory. It was upstairs in his bedroom underneath his T-shirts in a drawer. Bolivia said she trusted him with it, even after he had opened Lucette's cage.

When the puzzle was completed, they sat around trying to think of things to do. Derek got a deck of cards and showed them a couple of tricks that he had learned from one of the kids at camp. Then they played poker, rummy, and war. Gradually, the afternoon passed.

Mrs. Dunn called out the window to them all. "How would you like me to order a pizza for the three of you for supper?"

"Great," said Derek, answering for everyone.

"I bet I could eat a whole pie by myself," he bragged to Bolivia and Rory.

"That's eight slices. You couldn't eat that much," said Bolivia.

"Yes, I could," Derek insisted.

"I could eat a whole pie, too," said Rory.

"I'm bigger than you," said Derek. "You couldn't eat as much as I could."

"Size has nothing to do with it," said Bolivia, taking Rory's side. "Some very big people have small appetites and vice versa."

"You're crazy," Derek said.

"Hey, Ma," Rory called to his mother, who

had come out into the yard. "Would you order two pizzas?"

"You don't need two," said his mother. "One is plenty. I've called the store, and they will deliver one in half an hour. I'm going to cut up some vegetables for you to eat with it."

She went back into the house. "Too bad," said Derek. "If we had two pies, I could eat a whole one and prove to you that I could do it."

"I've got an idea," said Bolivia.

"What?" asked Rory and Derek.

"Let's order a second pie with our lemonade money."

"That's a great idea!" said Derek.

"No fair," said Rory. "I could eat a whole pie, too."

"You guys are both crazy," said Bolivia. "I bet neither of you could eat a whole pie, but I'm willing to let you try. I know that there'll be plenty left for me."

"Are you sure you want to risk that?" asked Derek.

"They'll be cold. That is, the slices that Derek doesn't finish. I know I won't leave any," said Rory.

"All right, show-offs. I'll go and call for the second pizza," said Bolivia. "I'll tell them to deliver it when they come, and I'll tell my aunt that I'm eating here."

She rushed into the house to make the call. Derek looked at Rory. "Where are you going to put all that pizza?" he asked him.

"In my mouth, the same as you," said Rory. He started clearing off the table. "We'll need this for eating on," he said. "You better go into my house and get the money to pay for the pizza." He instructed Derek where to find the money in his room.

By the time the delivery truck pulled up forty-five minutes later, Mrs. Dunn had brought out napkins, a pitcher of grape juice, and a plate of carrot, green pepper, and celery sticks. Neither Rory nor Derek touched any of the vegetables. They were saving room for the pizza.

"Two pies?" asked Mrs. Dunn when the delivery boy came up the walk with two boxes. "There must be a mistake. I only ordered one."

"Dunn, 26 Dogleg Lane?" said the fellow. "It says two pies here," he said, holding out a slip.

"The second one is mine," said Bolivia, rushing forward to pay with the lemonade money that Derek had given her.

"You'll never be able to eat all that," said Mrs. Dunn sharply.

"It was my idea," said Bolivia apologetically. "I made a bet with Derek and Rory."

Rory knew that even if she were annoyed, his mother wouldn't scold Bolivia. He was right. Instead, she said, "Edna is having scrambled eggs for supper because I'm fixing chicken livers for Mr. Dunn and myself. If there is a slice left, she would love it."

"There won't be any left," said Rory.

"Sorry, Mrs. Dunn," said Derek.

"I'll bring it inside to her," promised Bolivia.

"Stop talking and open the boxes," said Rory. "The pizza will be cold."

There wasn't room for two pizza pies on the card table.

"I can rest my box right on the ground," said Derek. "It will be empty in a few minutes anyhow."

"Okay. On your mark, get set, go," shouted Bolivia. She reached for a carrot stick and began chewing on it as she watched the competitors.

"I'm sorry that you won't be getting any, Bolivia," said Derek, chewing away on his first slice. "I'm really going to pig out today."

"Don't worry about me," she told him.

"No fair, Rory," said Derek, pointing to the crusts that his friend had thrown into the box as he grabbed his second slice.

"I never eat those," complained Rory. "They're too boring."

"That's cheating," said Bolivia. "At least, in an eating contest. I never eat them either."

Derek reached for his third slice. He was getting thirsty, so he stopped for a minute to gulp down some juice. He took a deep breath. "This is living," he said. "Imagine. Some people prefer chicken livers!"

They all made a face.

Rory wiped his fingers on his shorts and reached for his third slice, too. "See. I'm keeping up with you," he said to Derek. "Even when I eat the crusts."

Finishing that, he reached for his fourth slice. It was the slice he always wanted and never could have. Unfortunately, it didn't taste quite as good as he had imagined it would.

Derek began eating his fourth slice, too.

"Maybe we shouldn't be such pigs," said Rory. "Derek, don't you think we should each donate at least one slice to Bolivia." He stopped eating for a minute. "She was the one who had the idea of selling lemonade."

"You're right," said Derek. "It's only fair." he pointed to the box on the ground. "Here, Bolivia. Take a piece of my pizza."

"Oh, I wouldn't think of depriving you," said Bolivia. She was chewing on a piece of green pepper.

Rory reached for his fifth slice. There were

still three more slices in the box. "Bolivia," he insisted, "fair's fair. You worked hard selling the lemonade."

"You forgot. We didn't sell any lemonade," said Bolivia. "Most of the money was the reward you got for finding Mrs. Tillinghast's coin purse. So by rights you should eat all the pizza." She smiled and crunched down on a piece of celery.

"Too many vegetables will make you too healthy," said Derek. "Have a slice of pizza. Please."

"The nicest thing about eating celery is that chewing it makes a good noise," said Bolivia, munching away.

"I guess lying around all day because of my broken toes has kept me from having my usual appetite," Rory admitted. He was still nibbling at his fifth slice. He wasn't certain that he would be able to finish it.

"Confess that you're full," said Bolivia.

"I'm not full. Are you full, Derek?" Rory asked.

"Nope," said Derek. He was holding on to his fifth slice, too. "But I sure am not hungry either."

"Well, maybe I will do you guys a favor," said Bolivia. She reached into Derek's box and took out a slice.

"Hey, what about mine?" asked Rory.

Bolivia took a slice from Rory's box and placed it on top of the slice she was already holding. The tomato and cheese from each slice stuck together and the plain crusts were on the outside. "I'm having a pizza sandwich," she said as she began eating the two slices together.

Even though she was eating two slices at once, she finished them quickly. But she didn't eat the end crusts.

"Hey, you're supposed to eat those," said Rory, pointing to the crusts that she put down on the table.

"Why? I'm not in the contest," said Bolivia. "Aren't you guys eating any more?" she asked. They both shook their heads. Bolivia fixed herself another pizza sandwich.

"Delicious," she said. "I like it better cold. That way I don't burn my mouth." She finished her second sandwich except for the crusts and reached for another slice.

"Aren't you going to make another sandwich?" asked Rory.

"Nope," said Bolivia. "The last slice is for Edna. I promised to save it for her." She began chewing away on her fifth slice.

"Well, I guess it's a three-way tie," said Bolivia, wiping her hands on a napkin. "We each ate five slices."

"Yeah? You didn't eat your crusts," pointed out Rory.

"That's right," said Derek. At least the honor of boys against girls should be kept intact.

"True," agreed Bolivia, "but you didn't eat any salad." She pushed the plate of vegetables toward Derek and Rory, but both boys waved her away. Neither had any room at all.

"Derek, take this slice inside to Edna," said Bolivia, "and I'll put these crusts to good use." She picked up the crusts from her five slices.

"What are you going to do with them?" asked Rory.

"I'm going to bring them to Lucette," said Bolivia. "In all her life she never had as many pizza crusts as she wanted. She's going to break her record tonight, too."

"Don't talk about pizza records," said Rory, who felt as if pizza were coming out of his ears. "I may never be able to eat again." But though his stomach and his toes hurt him, he felt very good. It was great to have friends like Derek and Bolivia.

12
Barbecue II

Mrs. Dunn had a hard time finding a moment when Rory and Derek were together and Bolivia was not with them. She wanted to ask the boys if they had any ideas about a good-bye present for Bolivia.

Rory shook his head. It made him sad to think that Bolivia was leaving. First he had hated her coming and now he regretted her leaving.

"How about a T-shirt?" suggested Mrs. Dunn when neither boy had any suggestions.

"That's a good idea," said Derek.

"No," said Rory. "I don't think so. Bolivia should get something more than a T-shirt."

"It should be something to tell her that you've enjoyed knowing her and you'll remember her even when she is gone," his mother explained.

Rory thought hard. "I've got it!" he shouted.

Just then Bolivia walked through the hedge. "What have you got?" she asked.

"Nothing you can see," he answered, turning red. "Just an idea." And he kept it to himself for the time being.

Mr. and Mrs. Golding were giving a farewell barbecue for Bolivia. They would be driving Bolivia to Newark Airport early the next morning where she would get a plane to take her home. Bolivia's parents had returned from Turkey and would be waiting for her.

Unlike the impromptu barbecue that the Dunns had given to welcome the red-headed girl to Dogleg Lane at the beginning of the summer, this was a bigger celebration, with many more guests. Mrs. Golding had invited several of her friends, including Mrs. Tillinghast, who again thanked Rory and Bolivia for finding her coin purse.

Rory's father was walking around with a broad smile on his face. He had gotten A's in both his classes. All three of the children thought it was funny that grown-ups got report cards just like kids.

When Mrs. Golding gave a party, she really gave a party, Rory decided. In addition to hamburgers and hot dogs, she was serving barbecued chicken. There was fresh corn on the cob, three kinds of salad, homemade blueberry pie, and a cake as well.

Rory's foot was still very tender. He could walk on it if he put most of his weight on his heel. However, it was awkward, and so he preferred to sit on a lounge chair off to one side and let everyone wait on him. Mrs. Golding brought him a plate with a bit of everything on it, and then a little later his mother did the same thing. Rory was up to it.

Derek came over and sat down on the grass beside Rory's chair. "Great chow," he said as he bit into a leg of chicken. "They fed us some awful stuff at camp. Some of it looked like dog food and some of it looked even worse than that. The funny thing is that we ate it anyhow. Complaining about the food was one of the activities at camp, like swimming or hiking."

"Maybe next year, I'll go to camp, too," said Rory thoughtfully. "It's going to seem awfully dull around here without Bolivia." He paused a moment. "Do you think she might come back?"

Derek shrugged his shoulders as his mouth was too full of food to answer. When he had swallowed, he said, "I guess it depends on her parents. Remember how we were going to pretend she wasn't here?"

"That's because we didn't know what she

was like. Ignoring Bolivia is like trying to ignore a hurricane."

Derek laughed. "Remember when we thought Lucette was her little sister?"

"Some sister," said Rory, rubbing his sore toes.

"This summer sure turned out differently than I thought it would," said Derek.

"It was serendipity," said Rory.

"What's that?" asked Derek.

"It means we found something that we weren't even looking for—a new friend named Bolivia."

"Hey, you guys," shouted Bolivia, coming towards them. She sank down on the grass. "I was never the guest of honor at a party before this summer," she said. "Now it's happened twice."

Rory grinned sheepishly. He remembered how he'd treated Bolivia the first time.

"I guess you'll be glad to get home to Ithaca," he said. "With the famous bridge and everything."

"Yeah. And probably next year you'll go off to some exciting, faraway place like Turkey or Israel or something," said Derek.

"Maybe," said Bolivia. "But this was my best summer yet!"

"Did everyone have enough to eat?" Mrs. Golding asked the trio.

"Loads," Derek assured her.

"He's still full from too much pizza," said Bolivia, laughing and poking Derek in the stomach.

"It's too bad that Bolivia has to leave us. Perhaps she can come for another visit during the Christmas vacation," said Mrs. Golding. "I told you you'd love Bolivia," she said to the boys.

"Did you really tell them that?" asked Bolivia. "You hardly even knew me," she said to her great-aunt.

"Well, I knew any relative of mine would have to be wonderful. And I was right," said Mrs. Golding.

"Mrs. Golding, there's one thing that you forgot to cook for this barbecue," said Derek suddenly.

"Oh. What's that?" asked their neighbor, sounding concerned.

"You should have made a turkey."

"Right," said Rory, laughing. "Gobble, gobble, gobble."

"Gobble, gobble?" asked Mrs. Golding.

Derek, Rory, and even Bolivia nodded their heads. "Gobble, gobble, gobble," they said in unison.

From the upstairs screened window in the Golding house they could hear the sound of Lucette imitating them.

"Gobble gobble," squawked the parrot.

"Poor Lucette." Bolivia laughed. "She's really confused. She's going to go home thinking she's a turkey!"

Derek ran into his house and come out with a flat box wrapped in fancy paper. "This is from Rory and me," he said as everyone gathered around.

As Bolivia turned her attention to the package, Rory and Derek removed the T-shirts they were wearing. Underneath they each wore another shirt that matched the one Bolivia found inside the box. All three shirts were bright green and had the same navy-blue lettering, which read:

BOLIVIA,
MORE THAN JUST ANOTHER
COUNTRY

"Hey, look," shouted Bolivia with delight. "This is great." But her smile got even bigger when she looked up from the box at her friends and saw that they were wearing shirts that matched hers.

"Triplets!" She laughed. "Unless Rory spills something on me, of course."

"Look," said Rory, pointing at Edna.

The little girl was standing nearby nearly bursting with excitement. She, too, was wear-

ing a matching shirt in her three-year-old size.

"How come I didn't get a shirt?" asked Mr. Golding. "I want to belong to this club, too. Is it hard to join up?"

"No," said Edna, and she showed off her newest accomplishment.

"It's a snap." And she actually made a tiny click when her third finger hit the palm of her hand.

ABOUT THE AUTHOR

JOHANNA HURWITZ is a native of New York, a graduate of Queens College and Columbia University, a children's librarian, the mother of two teen-agers, and the author of fourteen books for boys and girls. Her humorous stories about Aldo, Nora, and Teddy and various other characters have made friends for her throughout the United States. In addition, several of the books have been published abroad in translation.

ABOUT THE ILLUSTRATOR

GAIL OWENS is a well-known children's book artist, living and working in Rock Tavern, New York. Among the many books she has illustrated are *The Cybil War* by Betsy Byars and *Hail, Hail, Camp Timberwood* by Ellen Conford.